---- ★ ----

It seemed to him, oddly, that he actually heard the blow after the pain, a distinct thunk, and his last clear thought was to wonder how that was possible. He fell sideways to the floor, and the numbness where the blow had struck began rapidly to spread through his head. But he did not lose consciousness immediately and so was able to feel recurrent blows to his body. These were not sharp, as the first blow to the head had been, but were massive and dull. He tried to raise his right arm protectively, but simply couldn't. Then the spreading numbness reached his eyes and closed down the light, and the next things that he was conscious of were the sounds of soft moaning, a continuing inability to move, and feeling very cold. He knew he lay like that for some time before he felt hands moving over his body and began to hear vague shouting sounds off in a distance.

---- ★ ----

# THE CARAVAGGIO BOOKS

## BERNARD PETERSON

**WORLDWIDE.**

TORONTO • NEW YORK • LONDON
AMSTERDAM • PARIS • SYDNEY • HAMBURG
STOCKHOLM • ATHENS • TOKYO • MILAN
MADRID • WARSAW • BUDAPEST • AUCKLAND

**THE CARAVAGGIO BOOKS**

A Worldwide Mystery/May 1997

First published by HarperCollins Publishers.

ISBN 0-373-26237-X

**Printed in U.S.A.**

To Sonya, who helped more than she knew

# ONE

JANET TWELVETREES had been living in the library for six weeks. In an uncharacteristically impulsive act she had broken off with Geoffrey Stephenson ('That's spelled G, E, O, Janet...') when he told her that her armpits smelled.

She had had a good situation living with him in his off-campus apartment. Air-conditioned in the summer and well-heated in the winter, it was on a tree-lined cul-de-sac only two blocks from the library where she spent so much of her time. He had rented the entire second floor of a vintage colonial frame house with wide-planked oak floors of a lustrousness that only wooden dowels and hundreds of polishings could produce. Geoffrey liked to live well, was generally easygoing, and was not at all reticent, physically or temperamentally, about sharing with her, although he would not, of course, permit her to contribute anything to his finances. And by and large she had had no real problem putting up with the one truly exasperating aspect of his psychological make-up—an attentiveness towards his person that, while falling short of narcissism, was clearly into hypochondria.

But she had been horny six weeks ago and play-

fully tried to jump him as he lay on the studio
couch deeply preoccupied by the fact that his father had just halved his allowance. And he had
rebuffed her. Only he didn't tell her that he wasn't
in the mood, or that he was thinking, or that he
had a problem. Instead he blurted out that her armpits smelled. And she, not knowing the real reason
for his rejection, fired back that his sensibilities
smelled. The situation quickly escalated into a recital of the most commonplace of mutual gripes,
but soon culminated in clenched fists, angry
breathing and glaring, resentful faces. The moment
came when they could very easily have burst into
laughter, put their arms about each other's waist,
and gone into the kitchen to fix dinner. But they
did not. Hers was the stubbornness of a fiercely
ambitious full-blooded Navajo, his was that of a
pampered, only-son, Eastern preppie. He told her
that if that's how she felt she could damn well
pack, and in five minutes she was on her way to
the first psychologically comfortable haven she had
known in her life, the Graduate Studies library of
Kingsford University.

And since she had no money for a place of her
own and she hadn't registered for a dorm room,
she wound up living there.

It was easier than anyone would have thought.
Since she was a doctoral student with an assigned
thesis topic ('Women in the Culture of the Plains
Indians') and a thesis adviser (Professor Maude
Greenberg, Women's Studies), she had a senior

study carrel all her own. For that first night she simply smuggled in her sleeping roll in an oversized Macy's shopping-bag, together with an onion bun, some yogurt and two pears. She stashed her suitcase at a friend's dorm room where she could change and shower but could not sleep since the ban on doubling up in rooms (whether with persons of the same or opposite sex) was one of the few genuinely enforced rules of the University. The easy success of the first night carried over readily to the next, and the next, and before she realized it she was continuing the practice almost without thinking. The only real drawback was a mild claustrophobia, but the moving air produced by a ventilator opening in the carrel went a long way to alleviate that. And besides, she quickly discovered that living in the library actually carried with it a great many conveniences. Before long she was into a really good groove on her thesis, carving out gratifying chunks at a rate that she reckoned would let her finish up in just one more semester.

But it was too good to last. One Monday night in midJune she had a large Coke with her roast beef and onion sandwich, and, sure enough, three a.m. found her on her familiar way to the toilet—past Russian History, right at Oversize Foreign Newspapers, and then ten yards past Photo-Dupe. Once again she acknowledged the con job she habitually performed on herself in believing that the library at three in the morning was definitely gloomier and more desolate than at three in the afternoon, although there were no windows at this level and the lighting never changed. She knew that the diurnal physical rhythms could be very strong and wondered if perhaps there were comparable psychological rhythms at work as well. Something to file away for the future, she thought.

She left the toilet and, since she was thirsty, took a drink at the water fountain by the elevators and so took a different route back to her carrel—through the large section on Literature of the Mediterranean three aisles over from her own. About half way along the corridor between rows of stacks on one side and a bank of graduate study carrels on the other, she noticed a dark wet smear on the floor that seemed to be seeping from under the door of one of the carrels. It was odd for several reasons: she had never noticed any puddles on the floor before, it was clear that even in the dim stacks lighting it was not water and, strangest of all, there was a strong animal odour about it. For a few seconds she just stood there before the puddle debating with herself what to do. Finally, because it was her way, she opened the carrel door, switched on the light to see for herself, and so discovered the body of Hilda Robertson sprawled over a typewriter with a slim-bladed knife lodged in the side of her throat. The shock of the sight froze her at first, but then the response mechanisms from her years on the Reservation in South Dakota surfaced and she quickly leaned forward to confirm by lack of pulse that she was dead, although that unique inertness peculiar to the dead had already told her that.

Her second response was much more personal; it was the rueful acceptance that, since she really had very little choice but to report this, her life in the near future was sure as hell going to change for the worse.

# TWO

THERE WERE FOUR of them, three of whom are arguably the most powerful men in Kingsford, seated around a conference table in Sam Dawson's office and all were hunched over as though deep in thought: Sam, the Chief of Police, whose thickening middle was becoming all too evident in the three-piece suit he was now wearing; Professor Gerald Waterston, the University President, in beautifully tailored charcoal grey; George Beliveau, Mayor of Kingsford, bleary-eyed, rumpled and unshaven in a checked polyester jacket; and Philip Constanza, the one and only detective on the Kingsford police force, in one of his five Ragg sweaters and six pairs of corduroys. Polyfoam coffee mugs sat before each of them. No one smoked, although Beliveau was fingering an open pack of Marlboros.

Dawson had been called at five, had picked up Constanza and Jim Morrall, the medical examiner, and had then spent half an hour at the library where they had supervised routine technical functions— initial examinations, photos, fingerprint dusting, and, finally, removal of the body to the hospital morgue and cleaning up the blood. Everyone had been meticulously careful to avoid unnecessary contamination of the scene. As the ambulance had driven away from the small crowd at the library entrance Dawson had leaned over to Constanza and murmured that maybe it would be a good idea to get together with Waterston and Beliveau as soon as possible and talk about this in private. 'Yeah,' Constanza had murmured back.

'I DON'T KNOW, Phil,' said Dawson, 'goddammit, I just don't know.'

'Exactly what, Sam?' said Beliveau. 'Exactly what don't you know?'

'Yes, Sam, it would be terribly helpful if you could clarify your feelings a bit here,' said Waterston.

Christ, thought Sam, how he hated that word. Terribly decent. Terribly considerate. Terribly affected, that's what it was. The people themselves were all right, most of them, anyhow. It was the goddamned way they talked. He'd been living in Kingsford for twelve years now and he'd never gotten used to it.

'Well, then, let me be as precise as I can,' said Dawson, deciding not to make his customary effort at being tactful. He took a deep breath for what he planned as a long sentence. 'What I am uncertain about is entrusting the investigation of this murder, which is going to be, at least for a while, a front page thing from the *Washington Post* to the *New York Times,* to one guy on a small town's police force who may have had lots of experience with breaking and entering, stolen property, and boisterous students, but zilch experience with full-blown, knife-in-the-throat murders.' Even with the deep breath, the sentence had been too long for one lungful of air. 'Now sure, this guy knows the town, has a good nose, and sports a Master's Degree in Sociology from Swarthmore, but I don't know if, in spite of all that, I shouldn't call in a team of detectives from Philadelphia to help out. It would give us manpower, big city technical resources, and—' he spoke slowly for emphasis—'an automatic out if there's a screw-up anywhere down the road. This could, after all, be a very hot potato.'

There was silence while this was digested. Constanza looked across at Dawson and spoke first. 'You know as well as I do, Sam, that a team of detectives from Philadelphia is not just going to help out here in Kingsford. They're going to run the show from day one.'

'I know that, Phil. Don't think I'm a total idiot.'

'I don't think that at all, Sam.' Constanza chose to ignore this perfect opportunity to mention Dawson's Phi Beta Kappa key from Temple, knowing that he, Dawson, would perceive this and accordingly be doubly chastised for his crack about Swarthmore.

'Yeah, I know, Phil. Sorry. I guess I'm a little upset.'

'If not downright cranky,' muttered Beliveau.

Dawson glanced at him expressionlessly, then

shifted away to Waterston and Constanza. 'To tell you the truth, I'm just not used to feeling uncertain, and I think it's making me uncomfortable.' Dawson made his smile simultaneously rueful and apologetic.

'And there are three or four good guys on the force, Sam,' continued Constanza, 'who also know the town and would be very good on a thing like this.'

'Yes, I know, Phil, but that doesn't change the nub of what I'm saying, does it?'

'No, it doesn't,' admitted Constanza. 'Not really.'

Beliveau shifted in his seat, looked first at Dawson and then at Constanza, and said, 'But if we decide to call in outside people on this right from the start, that's going to say that you guys are admitting that you can't cut it. That as professionals you just aren't up to it. And nobody likes to do that, right? Correct me if I'm wrong.'

Nobody spoke.

Waterston cleared his throat. 'Well, ah, let me understand something here. Chief Dawson, are you saying that this team of detectives from Philadelphia that you're thinking about, and Philadelphia's forensic resources, certainly more extensive than Kingsford's, would do a better investigating job than your own? No disrespect intended, but isn't that what we want? The best possible job?'

'Well, it's not quite that straightforward, Professor Waterston,' said Dawson, trying to match Waterston's tone. 'More and bigger are not necessarily better in a case like this. We're a small community and the Philadelphia detectives would suffer from a total ignorance of that community. That's a big handicap. Furthermore, just throwing more people at an investigation doesn't guarantee better or faster results. Sometimes, a well-aimed rifle shot is more effective at breaking open a lock than a load of buckshot.'

'Ah, I see,' said Waterston.

'And again, furthermore,' continued Dawson, 'we might quickly lose control of the shape of the investigation. A lot of extraneous trampling about might take place, and we might not want that to happen.'

'I'm sorry, but I think I'm beginning to lose you again.' Waterston was frowning now. 'Aren't we, in fact, beginning to drift a bit here? You see, I understand very well your remark about the preference of a rifle bullet to buckshot. However, I do not believe I completely understand the significance of your remark about a small community. Nor am I sure about what you mean exactly by trampling about. I should think that we ought to be concerned primarily with the solution to this horrible murder. But instead you seem to be off on a tack that I'm just not getting.'

'Professor Waterston, listen,' said Dawson, leaning forward. He chose words and tone carefully. 'A swarm of detectives from Philadelphia has potential ramifications you should be appraised of.

For one thing, they would be accompanied by an equally large swarm of reporters asking their own questions and making their own investigation. We're going to get some of that anyhow, but we would be well-advised to limit that sort of thing as much as possible. Delicacy and a finely judged sense of propriety are not a reporter's strong points, and in a short while I'm afraid a lot of dirty linen could begin to show that in purely objective terms would be counter-productive to the most effective investigation.'

Waterston was looking at Dawson with a small quizzical smile that seemed to indicate only partial comprehension, but that he was listening. Dawson decided to get it all out while he had his attention. 'Professor Waterston, there are certain routine goings-on at a university that you—we—might not want to have aired. There is a certain amount of backbiting, resentment of passed-over promotions, tenure fights, budget fights. These are things that are really quite commonplace at a university like Kingsford. But it is highly likely that some of these will come out, and in a very uncomplimentary way. Relevance is not necessarily a factor to the Sunday Features editor of the *New York Post*. Detectives may feel that what History Department secretary is shacking up with what Economics professor does not figure in this murder, but a hungry reporter is not going to be so objective.'

'Ah,' said Waterston softly. 'Yes. Now I'm beginning to see. Yes.' His eyes strayed to the window and the blossoming dogwoods just outside it.

'And one more thing,' intervened Constanza, 'that in a way bears on this subject. It addresses the question of community you mentioned before. You see, we're dealing here with a murder of someone in a lockable room on the fourth subterranean level of a building with very tightly controlled security and access. You need a Photo ID to get into the library, right, Professor?'

'I don't exactly comprehend the meaning of what you're saying,' said Waterston, a little testily. He was beginning to feel a bit irritated. He wasn't used to saying, 'I don't understand' so often.

'He means,' interrupted Dawson in a kindly tone of voice, 'that there is already an arrow pointing to the fact that the murder may have been done by someone with a Photo ID. I'm talking, Professor, about student *or* faculty.'

This time Waterston actually nodded. 'Yes,' he said again, 'I do see,' only more softly now, almost dreamily.

It was a lot to throw at him all at once like that, and both Dawson and Constanza waited considerately for him to respond. Waterston was clearly getting a lot more than he had bargained for. After the initial shock and then the mustering of his faculties (there had, in fact, never been a murder at Kingsford University), he had readily agreed that a meeting with the Police and the Mayor was a good idea. However, he had thought that it would be at most a polite briefing of sketchy facts, how best to inform the right people, and perhaps an initial press release. Instead he had been treated to a full-blown seminar on the pros, cons, and subtleties of various approaches to even an initial investigation, plus a concrete indication that the killer might actually be part of the University community.

For a time no one spoke. Waterston suddenly turned to the Mayor. 'You've hardly spoken, George. Surely you have some words on this matter.'

'Well, fewer than you might think, Gerald. I see a lot of my job here as representing the town's interest, and this is beginning to feel more and more to me like a University matter. This town has always been an adjunct to the University, Gerald. Kind of the tail that's wagged by the University dog, know what I mean? Very often we get included in University needs and affairs only as a matter of form. Hell, this isn't a complaint, Gerald. Considering how things have developed since you guys got your charter and your land, I guess it was inevitable. And the local merchants have no complaints about Parents' Day and Homecoming Week.' He shrugged. 'Sure, if the town gets involved in this thing directly, it may reflect poorly on the town, but right now I don't see it that way. I see it mostly as a University thing. So I don't have much to say at all, Gerald.'

George Beliveau suddenly glanced down at the

pack of cigarettes in his hand, slowly withdrew one and lit it.

'Yes,' said Gerald. 'Quite right, I suppose, George. Quite right.' He turned to Dawson. 'Mr Dawson, I'm getting the feeling that you and I are going ultimately to decide this question, indeed *should* be the ones to decide it, eh?'

Dawson nodded. 'And Constanza there, Professor. If we go with ourselves, he's going to be the main man.' This was Dawson's black, inner-city argot that he occasionally injected into the intellectual and genteel life of Kingsford. People who heard it usually attributed it either to a well-mannered attempt at shock or some sort of perverse charm. Constanza, who felt he knew him better, guessed it was more in the line of a small payment to his conscience, to assure himself that in allowing himself to accept the post of Police Chief of Kingsford, he had not gone completely white.

'Please, Chief Dawson, just one thing more,' said Waterston. 'Why do you necessarily suspect— expect—that discomforting circumstances may come to light during this investigation?'

'Part of my job is to suspect that, Professor. Even if I do not exactly expect it. Right?'

Waterston nodded. 'Right.' He was the only one who was not conscious of the wordplay being performed now, nor did it occur to him that for the last few minutes *he* was the one being patronized and manipulated; it was usually the other way around.

They were all looking at him now, but he didn't keep them waiting long. After all, he thought to himself, he wasn't the President of Kingsford University for nothing. All the time he had been looking dreamy and asking inane questions he had, of course, been thinking and weighing, as befitted both the academician and the Chief Executive Officer. And now he had decided (as though he had had—had been given—any other choice). He cleared his throat and put his right hand on the table. 'And just to save ourselves the time it would ordinarily take to arrive at what we would ultimately persuade ourselves had been a rationally and logically worked out conclusion,' he intoned, 'let's admit right now that, barring anyone's last-minute objection, it is agreed that at least for the moment we will be conducting the investigation ourselves.'

Waterston allowed a reasonable time to elapse, then turned to Dawson and said, 'And now, Mr Dawson, suppose we retire to my office and draft a release for the news media. I myself shall see to the notification of the poor girl's parents.'

# THREE

THE LIBRARY WAS IMMENSE, granitic, and shamelessly modelled after the one at Caius College, Cambridge. It was five storeys above ground, four storeys below ground, and, with its surrounding landscaping, covered five acres. The building itself looked as though it clearly belonged there, had sprouted and grown to be an ineluctable part of the land just as the trees and wild rhododendrons had. The ivy that grew up its walls started with a five-foot ground swathe on the surrounding lawn. The quarry stone of its outside walls was studded with tiny natural facets whose reflected light occasionally brought a shimmer of soft, multi-hued colour to its surface, especially under the oblique sun at dusk.

The library had fifty-eight miles of open stacks and, counting all its special collections, over ten million separate items on file. Almost three hundred people were employed by the library, but only one, its titular and tenured head, was officially part of Kingsford University's faculty. It had its own security system, its own parking lot, and its own generator for the power failures that occurred regularly during the spring and summer thundershowers. Its entrance atrium was sixty feet high. Its main reference and reading room had not one but two rings of balconies, one atop the other, holding most of the significant reference volumes and encyclopaedias of the Western World, and several of the Eastern. It had even more on microfiche. Next to salaries, its single largest expense item was the electricity that ran its lights and air-conditioning. It had fifty-two duplicating machines and one hundred and sixty-one fire-extinguishers. Its reference facilities were completely computerized, and while it took twenty seconds to simply check out a book, it would also tell you in those same twenty seconds what libraries in the United States carried the *New Delhi Times* for 1907. The library did not have any medical staff of its own, but it did have posted on every floor a list of those library personnel trained in cardio-pulmonary resuscitation and where they could generally be found. The practice of sex of any kind by students or faculty in any of the fifty-six study carrels was strictly forbidden, but it was well known that nobody had ever been expelled for having been caught at it.

The library's administrative assistant had given Philip Constanza a small office between the main Photo-Dupe room and the chief cataloguer's office. It contained a table, three chairs and, for some reason, a tea cart. No desk, no file cabinet. Two windows looked directly out over the main campus quadrangle where occasional movement and colour could always be counted on as a comfortable visual backdrop for the absorbed mind. At ten minutes to eleven a between-class break began and Constanza watched as the individuals and couples dotting the landscape grew to groups and streams. Purpose could be felt in their movements now. There were schedules to meet and demands to satisfy. The energy was palpable. Questing and focused, the students were cutting their aggressive paths through the courses of this University that, as was only proper for a first-rank Eastern-seaboard institution, functioned to satisfy such diverse ambitions as money, professional career, esteem, and the transplanted hopes of parents. There were some scholar-students, but they were in the minority. In the distant past, one had needed, for admission, money and the good fortune of having fathers who were alumni. (Being male was one of the admission requirements.) In the distant past, fully one-third of the student body were the offspring of such parents, and tuition bills were paid in advance and in one payment. Now, however, one-third of the students were on financial aid, the school was coeducational, and tuition, such was its magnitude, could be paid in quarterly instalments. There was an office of sexual counselling on campus, and it was considered bad taste to have only blacks serve at social functions. The old-time alumni were generally either perplexed or disappointed at the changes that had taken place over the last twenty-five years.

'Am I the first?' asked Janet Twelvetrees, choosing a chair facing the windows.

'Yes,' said Phil.

'Because I found the body?'

'Yes, again.' He motioned towards a couple of cans of Coke by way of invitation. He had brought them himself, forgetting napkins but remembering straws. 'I hope you don't mind the tape-recorder, Miss Twelvetrees. It really is a big convenience for me, letting me not have to take notes, but if it puts you off I won't use it. By the way, my name is Constanza, Phil Constanza, and I'm on the Kingsford police force. Detective-Sergeant.'

'How many don't like it?' she asked, nodding towards the tape-recorder.

'Oh, about half.'

'That many?'

'Yes.'

She nodded. So far they had both studiously avoided the fact that they were dressed almost identically in sweater, jeans, and sneakers. They both even had shoulder-bags, although Constanza's was larger.

Janet Twelvetrees had braided her long black hair into two strands that ran down from the sides of her head in Indian style. She was feeling a little insecure about the occasion, and wanted a sign, if only to herself, of her identity. The only other time she had done that was when she was asked out on her first date in Kingsford. 'Shall I start right in,' she said, 'or do you ask questions and I answer?'

Phil could detect no inflection of sarcasm, and simply chalked it up to the matter-of-factness that he saw in so many students these days. 'Suppose we just start right in, OK?'

'OK.' She glanced out the window, took a breath, then looked back at Constanza. 'Well, the fact is I'd been living in the library for about six weeks, sleeping in a sleeping-bag in my study carrel at night and working there on my thesis in the daytime. I had broken up with my boyfriend, a guy named Geoffrey Stephenson who lets the second floor at 11 Oak Tree Lane, and had no dorm room of my own. So I just started sleeping in my carrel, in a sleeping-bag, and nobody seemed to catch on. So I guess I just kept on doing it. It was working out just fine, too, I was getting along real well on my thesis and all.' She paused to give Constanza a chance to delve into any of what she'd said so far. But Phil chose not to interrupt. Her sleeping in Tavistock Library was odd all right, but not really his concern and he didn't want to get off on any tangents just now. She went on: 'Except that I often have a pint of milk or a soda late at night, and that means I usually have to go to the john about two or three in the morning. Well, that's what happened last night. I went to the ladies' room along aisle B and returned along aisle D— no special reason for that, just happened to use the water fountain near the elevators. Well, on my way back I noticed some dark liquid in the aisle. I guess I stopped, looked at the floor and I saw this large puddle and it looked funny. I mean, out of place, right? On a library floor? And it didn't look like water. Also, it smelled a bit. You know, a funny kind of animal smell. Hard to explain. Anyway, I looked down and it seemed to come from under the door of a study carrel and that looked funny, too. So I tried the door, and found it unlocked. Well, I sort of opened it a bit—'

'Excuse me,' said Phil. 'About that animal smell. I mean—'

'I don't mean like a dog or a cat. I mean more like when I was growing up. On the Reservation. Like passing a still fresh deer carcase hung up to dry, that kind of animal smell.'

'Right. I see. And now opening a door with a stain coming from under it. Wasn't that a little scary for you? I mean, in a dark library at three in the morning?'

'Well, yes, it was, a little. But it was unusual, and it caught my attention, I guess, and I suppose I didn't want to walk away from it not knowing. You know?' She had geared herself, on the way to the interview, to telling the truth. At least for a start, anyhow.

Phil looked at her. 'Is that your habit, Miss Twelvetrees? Not to walk away from things?'

Janet Twelvetrees paused. It was almost an intimate question and she wasn't prepared for it. Her response was automatic. She became wary. 'Well, sometimes yes, and sometimes no,' she said, sliding her eyes off Constanza to the Coke in her hands.

Phil silently berated himself for his clumsiness, and said 'Right. I'm sorry, please go on.'

'Well, so I opened the door and put the light on—it was dark—and I saw this girl slumped over the desk, a lot of blood all over her side and her arm and coming out of her open mouth, and you knew right away from all the blood and the look she had, slumped over that way, that she was dead. Also, I could see that knife sticking in her throat with the point coming out the other side. I touched her arm to feel for a pulse and there was none. It was the only thing I touched. I immediately went to the security station on the main floor and got a guard and we went back to the dead girl and he made a few phone calls and soon that black guy came over. You know, the one everybody was calling Chief, and he took charge.' She stopped talking and looked up. 'And that's just about it, I guess.'

Phil was a little taken aback by the emotionlessness of her recital. He tried to look noncommittal, but felt he was only partially successful. 'Uh, anything else? Where did you go afterwards?'

'Well, the black guy said to hang around, that he would probably want to have some detailed interviews later. I told him where I would be and went back to my thesis.'

Jesus Christ, back to her thesis?

'Did you know the girl, Miss Twelvetrees?'

'No, I didn't. Who was she, by the way?'

'An assistant professor in the Art Department. Hilda Robertson. Recently appointed.'

'She looked young.'

'She was. Twenty-five, I think. Master's Degree from Penn State.'

'Master's Degree? Is that all? And an assistant professor in a place like this? She must be pretty good.'

'Yes,' said Phil distantly. He suddenly turned towards her, frowning. 'Miss Twelvetrees, how many dead people have you seen in your life?'

The question was unexpected and brought her up short. She blinked once, then, frowning, moved her eyes from Constanza to a far corner of the room for a few moments.

She had, in fact, seen fourteen, ranging from a stillborn infant cousin, to her uncle Jimmy who, at ninety-six, had become fed up with all his physical infirmities and decided to 'pass over'. They included an inexperienced white hunter mauled to death by a mountain lion, a middle-aged couple poisoned by insufficiently diluted alcohol in their homemade gin, two people sentenced to death by the Council and publicly shot for a particularly brutal murder, the murder victim (put on display to justify the Council's action), and about a half dozen people killed in assorted brawls originating mostly in frustration and a somehow plentiful supply of cheap alcohol that came in from the outside.

Janet Twelvetrees's upbringing had accustomed her to seeing death almost as a normalcy and not particularly as something restricted to the old. It was not until she left the Reservation, in fact, that she discovered otherwise. And it was not until she entered Kingsford University that she learned that the rampant unemployment and alcoholism, the lack of any economic stimulus, was largely a consequence of governmental attitudes in general and the Bureau of Indian Affairs in particular.

One of the dead had been Charlie Whiteshoes, who once or twice a week regularly got drunk and beat up his wife. One night while he was sleeping after a particularly bad session, Mrs Whiteshoes had picked up the sharpest knife she could find, pulled his head back over the edge of the bed and, with a sinewy right arm, slit his throat to within an inch of decapitation. She then reported herself to the Council for judgement. (Janet Twelvetrees was fifteen at the time, had already been raped twice, and all she had even gotten from the Council was the advice to get married as soon as possible.) The Council was leaning towards turning Charlie Whiteshoes's wife over to the Dakota State Troopers when the oldest of them pointed out that she was his housekeeper, and if they did that he would lose her and well, he had gotten used to her. So they decided to do nothing. It was this series of events more than anything else that brought home to Janet Twelvetrees to what degree men's physical and psychological convenience would dominate her life on the Reservation. One week later she kissed her mother goodbye, took the bus into Fargo 'to see a movie', got a job as a waitress, found a room in a boardinghouse and entered South Dakota's public school system. When she phoned to tell her mother she wasn't coming back, all she got was a dreamy, 'Take care o'yourself, honey.' Well, she had done just that.

Janet Twelvetrees brought her eyes back to Constanza. 'Two,' she said, 'not counting Professor Robertson.'

'Tell me, Miss Twelvetrees, do you know anything about the Art Department, either through courses or friends? Anything like that?'

'No, not at all. And never have had since Art Appreciation 101 in undergraduate school.' She smiled slightly. 'I guess I'm not much help so far, am I?'

He smiled back. 'Well, we really don't know yet. Sometimes there's no telling what might have been helpful until we look back on it.' Christ, he hoped he hadn't sounded patronizing.

For a second he just looked at her. Her smile had changed the whole comportment of her face, emphasizing her broad cheekbones and the shine in her clear, widely spaced eyes. And the eyes were really black, a truly striking offset to their whites. He had never seen eyes like that.

'Tell me, Miss Twelvetrees, just what is the procedure for obtaining your Photo ID?'

'Well, you go to a small office in the Security Section and they have a regular tripod camera set-up, and they take your picture. It's a polaroid so they develop it right away. Then they type in your name, address, ID number, school, and then you sign your name and they encapsulate the whole thing in plastic while you're there with some machine. And that's it.' She paused. 'As far as I know, the staff and faculty go through the same procedure, if that's any help.'

'I see,' he said. 'Yes, thanks.'

She looked at him levelly. 'That was because anybody, no matter who, needs a Photo ID to get into the library in the first place, right?'

Constanza couldn't help smiling. 'Absolutely right, Miss Twelvetrees.'

He shifted around in his seat, moved his legs under the table and wound up hunched forward. If the table had been narrower, and they were sitting in a diner, the gesture could have indicated some degree of intimacy between them. But it was a large conference table and his leaning forward merely seemed to invite a lessening of formality. 'Now, Miss Twelvetrees, I'd like you to take your time on this next question, and please answer in any way you want to, even intuitively. When you got the door to the carrel open and saw the body, and realized what had happened, and got over that shock, was there anything, anything at all, that struck you as odd or out of joint, something that registered as somehow off-key? I know it may sound funny but you know what I mean, don't you?'

'Yes, I know, Mr Constanza. I know exactly.

And you know, there was.' She frowned with in-
tensity and Constanza noticed that the shape of her
eyes changed, from smooth ovals to a combination
of curved and straight-line segments. 'There was
no sign of a fight, or even of a struggle. I mean,
the papers were still all neatly piled up, the books
open and in place, pen and pencils on the desk,
nothing on the floor. There was no thrashing about,
you know? I mean, you wouldn't expect something
like that, right? Here's this girl, working away, she
looks up suddenly and sees this guy, and there's
no panic, not even much surprise. I mean, she
knew him, right? Or, at least, recognized him.' For
a moment she had actually become agitated, but
then quickly subsided. She blushed slightly. 'Sorry,
I didn't mean to come on so strong. But you did
ask.'

'Not at all, Miss Twelvetrees. That's just the
kind of answer I was looking for. And it was very
good of you to notice that.' Christ, was it that obvious to everyone? It was a cinch the reporters
were going to pick up on that. It'll probably be a
matter of just a day or two before faculty, students,
housewives, real-estate agents, the Acme checkout
clerks, the whole damn town is going to know that
Professor Hilda Robertson had a knife stuck in her
throat by either a student or a faculty member
whom she knew well enough that seeing him at
midnight in a deserted library apparently caused
her no anxiety.

'I notice you said "him", Miss Twelvetrees. Any reason for that?'

She blushed again. 'No, I should have said "person", I guess.'

'No problem. Tell me, is there anything else you can think of?'

'No, I don't think so. Not right now, anyhow.'

'Right. If you do, please call me, OK?' He fished a card out of his wallet and wrote something on the back. 'Here's my card. I've written my home phone number on the back. You can call me anytime.'

Janet Twelvetrees put the card in the small purse slung over her shoulder. 'I certainly will, Mr Constanza. Are we through now?'

Constanza sat back in his chair, stretched out his legs under the table and pulled his sweater down over his waist. 'Well, just one more thing, Miss Twelvetrees.' He paused, pulled at his lower lip, sucked at a tooth for a few seconds. 'Look. You've just discovered the body of a murdered girl. In a short while people are going to know that. Friends, acquaintances, and, starting very soon, reporters and people reading newspapers. You may be bothered a little by them. Maybe a lot. You may get peculiar mail, peculiar phone calls. People are funny. You know what I mean?'

Janet Twelvetrees did not frown or look puzzled. Her face was serious. 'I guess,' she said. 'Yes, I guess so. Also I suppose the University won't let me live in the library any more, but give me a regular room of some kind. So I might be easier to locate, right?'

'Right. Anyway, if things get really heavy, give me a call and maybe we can give you a hand, work something out with a rented room or something like that, OK? I can always fix it up with the University.'

She didn't know exactly what he had in mind. She could tell from his eyes that he had noticed her looks, and she wasn't sure if this was all in the line of business. He was wearing a wedding band, but that wouldn't necessarily make that big a difference. And with a sweater and jeans he wasn't at all what she had expected for her first police interrogation. People were funny, all right.

'Well, anyhow, thanks very much,' she said with a careful smile that she hoped was neither too much nor too little.

Constanza rose as she left the room.

The interview hadn't supplied any answers, but he really didn't expect it to. Some good questions were beginning to formulate, though. The first one was motive, of course. That had to be pursued immediately. But another one popped into his head and this one wasn't so straightforward. How did the murderer happen to be at a specific time and place, eleven or twelve o'clock at night on the fourth underground level, at a particular carrel, when Hilda Robertson would be available for murdering. Assuming that his presence was no accident, and that he was there to kill that particular person, how did he know that *she* would be there? Tracking her for any length of time, hanging around the carrel area waiting for her to show, could easily arouse suspicions if noticed. And it was common knowledge that security forces periodically patrolled library areas like that, even if only at three- or four-hour intervals. Unless, of course, it were all pure happenstance, if the guy just wanted to kill and Hilda Robertson was just unlucky enough to be around at the time. Well, the time of the murder might be consistent with that, but the very limited and well-defined group of people who had access to the library posed a built-in risk and made spontaneous murder very unlikely. Still, you could never really tell. Motive, if one existed, was what was needed now, and the quicker, the better.

Constanza suddenly realized he was hungry. He made a half-page of notes for himself on a steno pad, packed up recorder pad, pen and pencil, and left. His bicycle was chained to a tree just outside a back door, and while he could always have an official car at his disposal, he preferred biking. He undid the lock, slung his shoulder-bag across his chest and over the shoulder, mounted up and started out along the bike path that would take him off campus at a convenient point for his run home for lunch.

He liked the bicycle. He enjoyed its immediacy, the one-on-one, between his mobility and the resources of his own body. He derived a pleasure, almost a delight, in the connection between his thigh muscles and his speed on different types of terrain. The steering was pretty much the same as that of a car; for both bicycle and car you turned your hands and you changed direction. But on the bicycle you were your own engine, your own source of power. Sure, there were the obvious disadvantages: speed, rain, the armour of the car chassis. But the experience of the bicycle was much more elemental, and he savoured that. He savoured, too, the feel of the wind, and the pull of his shoulder-bag as he turned. He was self-contained on his bicycle, with all the identity and discipline that that implied. He was content to be on his bicycle.

But on the way home, he wondered, and not for the first time, if all his bicycle riding wasn't really some unconscious desire for a publicly recognizable eccentricity. Philip Constanza was genuinely suspicious of his subconscious and occasionally liked to call it to account.

# FOUR

HIS WAY HOME took him past several town land-
marks that in one way or another covered much of
Kingsford's history: the two-hundred-and-eighty-
year-old sycamore at the northwest edge of the
campus; the first traffic light installed in 1919 at
Kings Road and Daley Square (there were now
four lights in Kingsford); the cemetery that held
the remains of one former vice-president along
with two senators and two governors; the first supermarket ever built in Kingsford.

The town itself had grown and developed in its
own quirky way. From its inception in 1821, it had
slipped directly and gracefully into a strongly gen-
trified, typically Southern town of its time and remained that way through the Civil War, the building of the Pennsylvania Railroad's main track lines
just four miles away, and World Wars I and II.
Kingsford could get away with this chiefly because
it was almost totally surrounded by the farmlands
of central New Jersey, and because for all the nine-
teenth and half the twentieth centuries it consciously chose to keep its own evolution isolated
from the mainstream of the nation's changing con-
cerns and values. Knowing a good thing, the rulers

of Kingsford preferred to keep it to itself, and for the longest time were singularly successful at it.

The hierarchy of the town had developed along almost pre-ordained social and economic lines, an upper class defined by the large university faculty interleaving the town's other professionals, a rather sparse middle class of modest shopkeepers and town functionaries, and finally, of course, the underclass that serviced these people, blacks and (mostly Italian) ethnics.

There was one major variation on this theme, however, which in time was to produce upheaval, namely, a seedbed of latent liberalism lying for the most part dormant as a bulb in winter but ultimately to flower in the moist loam of post-World-War-II social activism. While the Civil War, and even World War I, left Kingsford's parochialism untouched in any concrete way, the town could not escape the onset of the crumbling of all sorts of class lines during the social refashioning of the post-war 'forties brought on by the GI Bill and the requirements of an enormous economic expansion.

However, the town was to weather the breaking of its societal moulds almost as gracefully as it had originally adopted them. After all, it wouldn't do for a university that prided itself on its liberal arts backbone to be, in the nineteen-fifties and -sixties, the central force in a town that did not change with the times. Indeed, said many, the University should lead the way. And so it did. Which was why it sold some of its extensive landholdings for affordable housing, dropped its rigidly administered admissions quota system (and substituted new 'affirmative action' ones), started admitting women and, finally, drastically expanded its financial assistance programmes. In time it became a highly visible model for enlightened socio-academic change, and sent faculty and town officials to lecture and consult on the complicated process of successful social change. In the final analysis, of course, it was what was to bring Janet Twelvetrees (member of two superbly visible minorities), Philip Constanza (son of an immigrant Italian stoneworker), and Sam Dawson (member of a black welfare family in Philadelphia) to Kingsford.

Philip and Sally Constanza lived in one of a strip of stucco-fronted, two-storey row houses three blocks from the main shopping centre. It was not considered one of Kingsford's most desirable locations. But a combination of Philip's finances and a genuine preference by Sally for just this type of environment for the children that she had wanted as soon as possible, had steered them to this neat and tidy middle-class street. Phil had had no objection.

Their Honda Accord was in the driveway with its trunk ajar. Phil closed it on his way into the house, entered without knocking and called out, 'Sally? I'm home, Sal.'

'Be down in a minute, Phil. There's beer in the fridge or put up water for tea, and there's chicken salad and hoagie rolls on the table.'

He had met her in a Route 1 diner eleven years ago; rather, he had seen her first in that diner eating with a group of giggling girls. He was driving back to Swarthmore from a party in New Brunswick and needed some coffee. He had looked around, as people do on entering a diner, and had noticed her immediately. She had well-defined, softly chiselled features with the sweetest jaw line he had ever seen, and her open, animated eyes shone at him all the way across the room.

He couldn't take his eyes off her and at the end, nervous as a boy at his first dance, he had simply waited for them to get up to leave and, as politely as he could and trying hard not to stammer, he had said, 'Excuse me,' tapped her on the shoulder, and asked if he could please call her sometime. Later, she told him that he *had* stammered a little but that the 'please' had been irresistible and, well, he was kind of cute. She had been eighteen at the time and it was two full years before they married. There had been some hostility from her blue-collar parents about his going to Swarthmore, which intensified when he enrolled in Graduate School. Sally was just about to start a thoroughly acceptable job at the local branch of Chemical New Jersey Bank, there were lots of boyfriends from around Edison where she lived, and the parents were concerned about losing their girl to this 'different' sort of fellow who might very well take her away, dilute her Catholicism, and expose her to ideas that would be different from theirs. But (and they were never to realize this) they were seriously underestimating their daughter's individuality. It developed that Sally and Phil were never to be more than an hour's drive from Edison, that Sally needed no outside help to dilute her Catholicism, and her ideas about life turned out to be only partially objectionable to her parents. Whenever Phil would talk to her about quitting the bank and starting college Sally would reply that no, she really didn't want that, that she was all right and really just wanted to love him and have a good family with him. For a time Phil was uncomfortable with having such an impact on someone else's life. But he loved her, and she him, and that's the way it was, and, finally, as far as he was concerned there was, after that, only one logical thing for him to do. There were friends of his who thought that he was making a big mistake marrying a high school girl from Edison, and that besides, he was too young. But Phil knew better. In any event, his waiting until he had gotten his Master's ('finished school') and then landing a job with the State Troopers helped everybody's feelings.

Becoming a 'cop' had been the last thing on his mind when he finally got his degree in Sociology. But by that time Phil and Sally had reached the point where they were talking intimately and freely about what was in their heads. One night he told her that rather than interacting mostly with the one group you either worked with or lived with, which was what he had most often seen happen, he liked the idea of dealing with many different types of classes of people. 'And I think I could do that well. I sort of like the idea of being significant in society in a helpful way. And one thing I found out in Grad School was that I don't like teaching much; it all seems so static and predetermined. I've been thinking that maybe I'd like to do political internships or maybe foundation work.' They were in each other's arms—they necked heavily but never made love until after they were married; it was the way she wanted it and Phil was too in love to force the issue with her—when she suddenly pulled away and blurted out, 'You ever think of becoming a policeman? You're strong enough and I'll bet with your college degree you could do really well there. With all those things you've talked about maybe you should think about that a little.' Phil had learned by this time not to pooh-pooh anything that Sally said, no matter how it sounded. She had too often pinpointed someone's personality trait after a party at Swarthmore, or said who she would or would not trust, and turned out to be dead right.

And she had been right about his being a policeman, too. He had indeed thought about it and, admittedly attracted partly by its piquancy, took the plunge and 'for a trial period' joined the State Police. Somewhat to his surprise he quickly found that he liked it, liked the initial schooling, found dealing with people in exigent situations—accidents, speedings, disputes, interrogations—gratifying and fulfilling. He did well at his duties and found his academic background in Sociology surprisingly applicable to his job. (Well, he would think later on, maybe not so surprisingly.) And he had been lucky in one very important respect; he had never had to fire his gun off the practice range. When his sergeant had pointed out to him the opening at the Kingsford Police Department, he applied and, with his credentials, was enthusiastically accepted—just as Sally had predicted. That had been six years ago.

She bounded into the kitchen. 'And there's some local strawberries I got just this morning. Say, wasn't that something about that poor girl who was killed? You're involved with that, right? I mean, you're Kingsford's detective, right? It's all over town. You interview anybody yet? Is Sam Dawson involved, too? Is there anything you can tell me yet?' She suddenly threw her arms around him, kissed him hard and pressed up against him and wiggled. 'C'mon, you can tell me.'

'Hey, take it easy, Sal.' He laughed. 'And, no, I can't tell you. No matter what you do.' He kissed her back and ran his hands over her hips. 'Well, maybe there are a couple of things you can do.' He let go of her, reached for a strawberry and popped it into his mouth. 'Not that there's much to tell, anyhow.' He started to make a sandwich. 'Talked to the girl that found the body. Don't even have a good motive, yet.'

'Oh,' she said brightly. 'Well, you know what Jessica Hamilton told me in the Acme? She said that Professor Beecham—he's the chairman of the Art Department—well, she said he was shacking up with that girl who was killed. Got her an apartment at Hoskins Hall way ahead of turn. His wife left him about six months ago, you know. Or maybe he left her. Well, anyhow, even though she was so young and didn't even have a Doctorate, he gave her an appointment in the Department— apparently department heads can do that—and got a lot of people upset, grad students, tenured people, a whole lot of people even outside the Department. And not only that, but that she was seeing some- body else. At least, people saw her at McCardle's with someone else, especially when Beecham was out of town. A black student, Jessica said. Any- how, at least he was a young guy. And everybody knew about it. But she was still living at Hoskins, see, and Beecham was visiting her a couple of times a week and—Philly, what's the matter? You look funny.'

Constanza had sat down limply, mouth open, half a hoagie roll in his left hand, mayonnaise- covered knife in his right, and was staring at her dumbly.

'Jesus Christ, Sal, what are you saying? Is all of that true? Where did you get all that stuff?'

'Well, as I said, Jessica Hamilton told me in front of the cottage cheese. You know Sarah Dom- browsky? Well, she does typing for the Art De- partment and she and Jessica are good friends and that's where she got all this. I'm sure it's true, Phil.

I don't think she would lie about any of this. I mean, given the circumstances. Are you all right? Should I stop, Phil?'

Constanza put down the roll and looked at her intently. 'Hon, now this is serious.' Then he grinned. He simply couldn't help it. The whole situation rang gongs in his head. 'Sal, don't you realize that you've just covered grounds for half the human behaviour in the world? Remember when I finally convinced you that all human conduct could be attributed to only four things? Well, you've just covered three of them. Hell, Sal, you've mentioned enough motive for ten murders.'

'Yeah? Which one did I leave out?'

'Well, you've covered love, sex and esteem in a hundred words or less. You left out power. And I'll bet that if I gave you another minute you'd mention something that would include that as well.'

Sally sat down opposite him, smiled happily, and leaned forward. 'Kiss me,' she said in a stage whisper, 'I love it when you get exasperated.'

'Listen, Sal, I think you're cute, too. But you really have to tell me if all this is true or if you made it up. I mean any of it, OK? It really is important information if it's true and—'

'No, I think it really is true, Phil. At least, it really is what Jessica told me. And I know that this may be hard for you to understand but the fact that Jessica Hamilton told these things to the wife of Kingsford's one and only detective puts the stamp of truth on it. No self-respecting gossip would dare tell such things if it were not accurate. She would have too much to lose. Reputation is at stake, here, Phil. You should trust me on this.'

Constanza nodded. 'Yeah, I guess I should. God, what a mind was lost to Psychology when you decided not to go to college.'

'I practise enough psychology with the kids. And it's all field work, too.'

'And with me?' Phil asked, smiling. 'Am I psychological field work, too?'

'Well, no more than what you practise. The thing is, you and I, we both know it when it happens. If we didn't, then there might be trouble. And besides, it's never anything really heavy, so it's really OK. You know what I mean? Besides, don't give up on me yet. When the kids grow up I may be one of those forty-five-year-old college graduates. Listen, finish making your sandwich so I can put the mayonnaise back in the fridge.'

Constanza did as he was told and half way through lunch Sally said she had forgotten to tell him that Sam Dawson had left a message that he wanted to see Phil at two o'clock.

# FIVE

IT WAS ONLY ONE O'CLOCK when Phil left, so he took the long route back to the Municipal Building that he knew from experience would take about forty-five minutes. It took him along the edge of what students called, with a vocal inflection that depended on social origin, 'Rich Man's Ghetto'. Here, lots had been zoned for one acre and contained ten-room houses, impeccably landscaped, that sold for three-quarters of a million dollars and higher to doctors and corporate executives commuting to New York and Philadelphia. During the 'sixties there had been a more or less symbiotic discovery among neighbouring potato farmers, aggressive real estate developers and affluent city dwellers: farmers could sell their land and become overnight millionaires, developers could fund their housing construction with low-risk borrowed money, and the affluent could exchange their Manhattan duplexes and their Historic Philadelphia townhouses for a much more gracious and spacious Kingsford lifestyle. A period of feverish building took place in which the Kingsford Town Council and zoning Board, which for decades had had relatively little to do, was suddenly catapulted into equally feverish activity. For the first time real tension developed between representatives of the University and the town, and while the University could, to some degree, shape the explosive expansion, it could not stop it. It could limit structures to three storeys and keep out industry, but it could not eliminate commercial zoning off the main streets or parking garages. Maintaining some semblance of rural graciousness was one thing; interfering with a burgeoning tax base and a veritable flood of money for shopkeepers and foodstores (and their employees) was quite another. It was roughly at this time that one former mayor, the owner of the local General Motors franchise, overstepped the bounds of acceptable hubris by publicly avowing that his goal was to achieve Kingsford's first traffic jam. He succeeded, but then was roundly defeated at the next election. The local newspaper remarked that the only reason a recall election had not been held was that it would have been considered vulgar. Such was the equivocal nature of the town's image of itself.

In time, of course, everyone came to realize that some cap should be put on both the population and the commercial growth, otherwise the changing character of Kingsford would soon lessen its attractiveness. This was handily accomplished by simply freezing new residence zoning at two acres, which at one blow both limited the number of new homesites and increased already existing property values. The Kingsford zip code became even more desirable and expensive to own, and the town, though somewhat less bucolic, still retained a mostly small town atmosphere. And if Kingsford was no longer totally dominated by the University, it was still the factor that brought small independent laboratories, corporate conference centres and executive training sites to the area.

The only group that took irretrievable and unforgiving exception to these changes was the landed, reactionary Old Guard who were upset at the influx of Orientals and Jews into both the University and the town, but about which they could do very little and not be literally hauled into court. As ever, they much preferred things as they had been.

Constanza pulled up to the bike rack, passed a chain-lock around the grate and through his wheel spokes, slung his bag over his shoulder and entered the Police Department's section of the building. He was fifteen minutes early and saw from the duty roster on the wall that Dawson had not yet returned from lunch. Constanza decided to go over his notes in the Mayor's anteroom which had much more comfortable chairs. One of Sam Dawson's first acts as Police Chief had been to get rid of the luxurious Italian leather armchairs his predecessor had ordered for his waiting-room ('I don't want people waiting to see me to be that comfortable') and had them replaced by something more institutional.

# SIX

CHIEF DAWSON was running late because he had lost track of the time. After the meeting with Waterston, Beliveau and Constanza, he had spent the next twenty minutes on the toilet dividing his attention between his haemorrhoids and making notes on a yellow legal pad on his lap. The remainder of the morning he had spent mostly on the telephone or the office intercom.

First, he spoke to Mary Underwood (MA Eng. Lit., Rutgers), his secretary, office manager and receptionist who was worth twice the salary the Township Board voted her every year, and told her to come into the office with her book. She was a soft-spoken, blue-eyed blonde from a small village in the pine barrens of New Jersey who, when complimented on her looks, liked to bat her eyes and smile sweetly before replying, 'Well, I've got good ass but really no tits to speak of.' She had earned the sobriquet Iron Balls (which she secretly loved) after knocking out a would-be mugger one night in New Brunswick with a wool sock containing three two-inch steel ball bearings. Sam Dawson admitted to very close friends that he would kill for her. Three days ago she had announced her engagement and imminent marriage to a Physics grad student three years younger than her own thirty, and only after he had congratulated her and hemmed and hawed for a while did she sigh theatrically and say that no, she was not knocked up and not planning on quitting any time soon, that someone had to earn some money to live on. Dawson had said he was glad on both counts.

Then he said, 'Listen, Mary, please type up a memo, no longer than half a page, addressed to "Members of the Press" to the effect that there will be a press conference today, Tuesday, the ninth, in the Colonial Room of the Kingsford Inn at six o'clock at which they will be brought up to date by me, my chief investigator and members of the University's security forces. Reporters' questions will be answered as best they can. Professor Waterston of the University will also be there. Uh, wait, better make that President Waterston. Then give me a blank page with a title at its head that reads, *Résumé of Developments in Ongoing Investigation.* I'll give you some stuff for that this afternoon. If you don't get anything from me by four o'clock, please remind me, OK? I want some of these at the Sergeant's Desk out front by five o'clock and another batch I can take with me to the Inn. And let me see the stuff before you run off final copies.'

'Don't I always, Chief Dawson?'

'Yes, you do, Mary. Sorry.' In some ways he

already felt sorry for that grad student. 'Anything for me this morning?'

'Well, you've already got four phone calls from reporters at the *Trenton Times* and the *New York Times*, the *Baltimore Sun* and the *Philadelphia Enquirer*. The one from Baltimore said he went to school with you.'

'Yeah, that would be Hal Jamison, right?'

'That's right, Chief. They all said more or less the same thing. They're on their way and want to talk to you as soon as they arrive. They all left phone numbers for you to call back on.'

'Sure, as though that's all I have to do here today.'

'I guess you're one step ahead of them, huh, Chief?'

'Well, it's not really all that hard, Mary. Sometimes it is, but not this time.'

She turned to leave, then paused, turned and said, 'By the way, how did they all find out so soon? I mean, it's only been a few hours since, uh, you know...'

'Well, once the homicide, or any major crime, gets logged in here, it automatically goes on to a data base that all modern police stations can hook into. All those newspapers you mentioned have reporters who specifically cover police business, and if they have any decent contacts at the station they get called right away. And a murder at Kingsford University, Mary, is not minor league stuff, I'm afraid.'

Mary Underwood said, 'Oh,' nodded and left. Dawson rubbed at his eyes, took a deep breath, and picked up the phone to call the Kingsford Inn's manager, Harvey Stanwood.

'Mr Stanwood, this is Police Chief Dawson... And good day to you, too, sir... Yes, it is a dreadful thing. Listen, I would like to book the Colonial Room for this evening at six o'clock on official township business for a press conference... Right, the bill to the Mayor's office... Yes, I know there are larger and pleasanter rooms all above ground with nicer views but I really would prefer the Colonial. In addition, I would like you to see to it that only one water-cooler is available in the room, that only wooden folding chairs are used in setting up, and that if anyone asks, there are no other rooms readily available... Right... A half-dozen chairs up front flanking the lectern would be fine... No, no refreshments, nibbles, or other gestures of hospitality... Right... Right...' Dawson smiled broadly. 'That's nicely put, Mr Stanwood. The number of available chairs I don't want exceeded is fifteen... Your understanding and cooperation are duly noted... Right. I appreciate that and I thank you, sir. Goodbye.'

Dawson replaced the phone in its cradle, waited a couple of seconds, then picked it up again and dialled Charlie Harris's private number at the *Kingsford Chronicle*. 'Hello, Charlie? Sam Dawson here. How are you?... Yeah, sure is... No, nothing yet... Yeah, well, a couple of things I could fill you in on. I've assigned Phil Constanza as the chief investigator. I'll be along for consultation and stuff, but I want our ranking detective to handle the nitty-gritty. He'll have first call on all Department personnel and resources and the investigation will have the number one priority of the Department... Right. We're convinced that given all the circumstances, he will have the best chance at conducting the most effective investigation possible... Right... Exactly. Knowledge of the town and the University, possibility that the perpetrator was an insider, the way things work in Kingsford, stuff like that. And, of course, if we ever need super forensics or lab work, there's always Philadelphia... Terrific. Thank you, Charlie.

'Uh, listen, Charlie, one more thing. I would appreciate it very much if I could see or know about any article in the *Chronicle* that might bear significantly on the investigation, something that might turn out to be sensitive even though it might not be thought so at the time... No, I mean beforehand, Charlie... Well, what I have in mind is some information about a likely or probable suspect, something that one of your bright young men—or women—might stumble across or speculate on, some commentary or editorializing that might work to adversely affect a police investigation. To be straight out, Charlie, sometimes not every piece of information we acquire or you acquire should go immediately into the public information hopper... C'mon now, Charlie, you know I'm not talk-

ing about censorship or prior restraint. I'm talking
about doing the best job I can... All right, yes, the
best police job, and, granted, one man's best police
job can be another man's censorship. So why don't
we both agree that each of us knows what the other
guy means here and... No, Charlie, I'm not afraid
of the possibility that we can be shown up or ed-
itorialized about by the local paper. In fact, you
guys have already done that to us in the past several times, right? There are a lot of people around
who think that that's exactly the way it should be
and, just for your information, I happen to be one
of them... Charlie, this is not a question of usurp-
ing prerogative or undermining the free press. It's
a question of reasonable cooperation in matters
of... Yes, I said cooperation... Of course I will,
Charlie. My local newspaper will always get priority on news releases of any significant developments. I will see to it personally... Not only do I
think it's fair, I think it's appropriate, valid and
desirable. Not only would I not mind the *Chronicle's* showing up the *Philadelphia Enquirer* or the
*Washington Post,* I would not even mind aiding
and abetting. Look, ultimately this whole thing
comes down to a matter of trust between... For
Chrissake, Harris, the mere fact that I'm saying
some of these things to you indicates the level of
my trust. You think I don't know what an accurate
but slanted write-up of this conversation could
sound like?... You're damned right it is... No, no.
No offence taken... Good... Terrific. I couldn't

have expressed it better myself… I appreciate it very much, Charlie. It'll really be a help. Thanks again. So long.'

Dawson hung up and sighed deeply. That took longer than he had thought, but tone was important here. It had all come out all right, though, and it never hurt to be on good terms with the press.

He had one more call to make. He dialled the main number at the University and asked for the President's office. A woman answered, and after he had identified himself and asked for Professor Waterston, he was told that the President was at a meeting and could not be disturbed. The voice was slightly affected, highly officious, and clearly originated from a woman very much taken up with herself. Dawson shook his head. Christ, what was it that made these people so defensive and insecure? A goddamned doctoral thesis could be done on it.

'You're Miss…?'

'This is Mrs Campbell.'

'Well, listen, Mrs Campbell, I'm afraid I'm going to ask you to interrupt that meeting, tell the President who this is and that I have to speak with him. I don't care if you tell him publicly or privately, although my feeling is he would not mind publicly. I don't care how important the meeting is. And you will do that now because the Chief of Police is asking you to and if you don't your judgement will be seriously, and publicly, questioned. I'll wait.'

Dawson waited patiently for a few seconds to allow Mrs Campbell some time to absorb all this and to weigh everything he had said. But the conclusion, Dawson had learned from experience in dealing with University functionaries, was foregone.

'Just one moment, please, Mr Dawson.'

In a short time Professor Waterston came on the line. 'Chief Dawson. How may I help you?'

'I'm very sorry to disturb you, Professor Waterston, but there was no telling how the rest of my day would go and I felt we should talk on a couple of items. First, I've reserved the Colonial Room at the Kingsford Inn for a press conference at six this evening. The reporters are already calling me and they have to have something. I'll be there, and so will Constanza. I suggest you be there, too, and perhaps your Chief of Security... I understand. In that event, by all means the one who speaks well and makes a good impression. Sorry, but yes, that may make a difference. Tell me, have you contacted the parents yet?... Yes... I see... No, it's never easy. From what you're telling me, I would guess you did extremely well... No, I'd be glad to be along when you meet them. Tell me, is the fact that I'm a black police chief going to present any awkwardness for you?' (This was said in the most matter-of-fact of tones. Dawson had long ago concluded that there were times when people's responses to his colour were best treated simply as facts of life and should be accommodated accordingly. But not always.) 'Fine... Well, Constanza has already questioned Miss Twelve-trees and I'll be seeing him in about an hour and a half. I'll certainly keep you posted. Incidentally, I'd appreciate your keeping everything I tell you about the investigation strictly confidential. We'd like to keep our plans, information and ideas from being general knowledge. I'm sure you understand... No, I've already spoken to Charlie Harris and we've come to an understanding... Ah, that's an excellent suggestion. A hand-out at the press conference of a résumé updating developments in our investigation would be very appropriate. I'll be glad to take care of it and also to be sure you see it before I release it... Not at all... You're very welcome... Right, we'll be in touch. Goodbye.'

Dawson hung up the phone, folded his hands at the back of his neck, arched his back and for a few minutes simply stared at the ceiling. Occasionally, a softly whistled melody escaped him. He tried to place it, but couldn't. A Mozart Piano Concerto, he thought. Or an aria. Hell, there's always an awful lot of aria in his concertos, anyhow. He tried to remember where he had heard it, but couldn't. He finally gave it up and walked to the window, opened it and put some birdseed from a box in the stationery closet on the outside ledge. After a while he walked back to his desk and sat down. Again, he put his hands to the back of his neck and turned his face to the ceiling.

The fact was that Sam Dawson had been antsy

for a couple of years now. It wasn't that he disliked his job. The gratifications were all there in decent measure; good acceptance by the important academic and town people, good rapport with the work force, enough visibility and power for a moderate ego, good enough pay. Most people in his profession would consider Chief of Police of Kingsford a plum. He knew that. He also knew that being black had been a factor—in this case a perversely positive one—in his being hired. But his antennae were very good and he felt that after twelve years his colour had now become, in the great majority of cases, an irrelevancy in his professional involvements. He only wished his mother had lived another ten years to see it.

No, the trouble was that the job was getting to be too easy. He was getting to be too good at it. It all came so effortlessly now. His clarity in doing his work was such that he could see almost immediately what was the right or appropriate thing to do in a situation. During all his years in Kingsford he had honed his sense of when to come down hard and when not to, when to lean on situations and when to back off, when to confront and when to outflank. For some time now he had made no major mistakes and few minor ones. He had developed, and now possessed to an extraordinary degree, that political schizophrenia of being able to put himself into his adversary's head while still keeping sight of exactly what was in his own. And he had used this talent to handle successfully the disparate elements of a highly visible academic-business-bedroom town just off the New York—Washington corridor.

He had also made some discoveries about himself. He learned, for example, to downplay his superior verbal skills at town council meetings when he began to sense that he was being resented for it. After all, this might be interfering with his effectiveness and, in his mind, interfering with effectiveness was almost sinful. He had come a long way in his job, in many dimensions, and was duly grateful for it. In fact, the only significant negative for Chief Sam Dawson was Mayor George Beliveau, whom he simply considered to be a dumb jerk; and it had been no great solace to him to discover that a lot of people connected with town government thought similarly. Dawson still had to deal with him, nominally, as his boss.

Sam Dawson was restive in his job because his job could no longer teach him anything, and so was no longer interesting to him. It was time he moved on. The question was, to where, or to what?

He hit the intercom. 'Mary, I'm going out to lunch. Get hold of Constanza and tell him to see me here at two o'clock, OK? I'll be at the Greek place.' He'd had enough of the carefully shaped language of university presidents and hotel managers; he wanted to hear some coarse ethnic talk and eat Greek salad with extra olives and wipe the wine vinegar and olive oil off his plate with warm pitta bread. But only single portions today; he didn't want to eat too much for lunch and risk getting drowsy later on. Not today.

He went out of a side door just to ensure not seeing anyone who might want to talk. Christ! A real, dyed-in-the-wool, big city killing. Who would ever have thought it at Kingsford.

He shook his head. That poor kid.

# SEVEN

CONSTANZA NODDED to Mary Underwood and followed Dawson into his office. The first thing you noticed about Sam Dawson's office was its neatness, the type of neatness that required effort. It signified the only hint of compulsive behaviour that Constanza had ever noticed in Dawson. While it was true that Dawson's desk was not clear, the several piles of paper on it were neatly stacked and lined up with the desk's edges. A central conference table, the same one used that morning, was completely clear. Three file cabinets and a stationery closet, all institutional grey, ranged along one wall with front edges perfectly aligned. A clean chalk board hung on the far wall directly opposite Dawson's desk with one clean eraser and two new pieces of chalk at the extreme left edge of the eraser shelf. Nothing was askew. Even the shadows produced by a midday sun slanting in through the windows made patterns of lines that paralleled the walls.

Constanza sat where he usually sat, under a side window, and while Dawson thumbed through the small pile of mail that Mary Underwood had allowed to reach his desk, looked around once again with pleasure at some of Dawson's things, placed so as not to conflict with the room's orderliness. As usual, he fixed first on the framed three by four feet blow-up of a photo of a lioness crouched in repose in tall grass, her strong yet completely feline head resting on crossed paws, and looking quizzically at the camera. A swishing tail had been caught apparently in mid-air. The sun was low and came from behind the camera so that ridges of muscle around the shoulders and along the ribcage were sharply emphasized. Constanza had never before seen so eloquent a depiction of the almost casual power of the jungle animal.

Only after the impact of the lioness began to dissipate did his eyes veer off to the smooth ebony bust, very cool to the touch, of a queen of ancient Egypt with its heavily stylized, almost liquid facial features. And then there were the birds, mounted along one wall near the ceiling. They were four in number, also of ebony, with highly streamlined shapes and with long necks completely extended in graceful flight, that seemed to Constanza to rival Brancusi in impressionistic suggestiveness.

'You still like the lioness, Phil?' broke in Dawson.

'You know I do, Sam. Doesn't everybody?'

'Interestingly enough, no. You'd be surprised at how many look at it, frown, then look away. Maybe they get intimidated. I don't know.'

'Maybe they look at it and get intimidated by you, Sam. Maybe they see it as an amplification of their response to you. Maybe that's why you hung it up there.'

Dawson made a show of seeming to study that. 'That's not bad, Phil. A little better, in fact, than your usual psychotalk. And if it were true, it would be a lot better.'

But you didn't outright say it was false, thought Constanza.

'You get anything from the girl?' asked Dawson.

'I don't think so, although she lied once.'

Dawson looked up. 'You mean, *at least* once.'

Constanza nodded. 'Right, Sam. At least once. It was about her time on the Reservation, but I didn't want to get sidetracked. One thing *was* brought home to me, though, and that is that anyone with a half a brain is going to realize that the killer almost certainly had a University Photo ID and almost certainly knew his way around the library.'

'She say that?' asked Dawson.

'Yes, she did.'

Dawson shook his head sadly. 'Shit,' he said. Then: 'You know, I really have this feeling that this is going to be a mess before it's over.'

Constanza nodded, then began to recount his questioning of Janet Twelvetrees. Dawson interrupted only once to comment that the Indian Reservations had been dumped on pretty thoroughly by the Government and he had heard that things could get pretty rough 'out there' in the wilds of the Dakotas. 'Not at all civilized, like how the white folks did it to the black slum ghettos of rural Mississippi,' he said. Constanza's eyes flicked up for an instant and then returned to his notes.

After he had finished, Dawson asked what Constanza's next move would be.

'Well, I'd like to see the carrel again.' He caught himself from saying 'the murder carrel'. 'It's still undisturbed, right?'

'Still pristine,' said Dawson. 'Except the body's gone, of course.'

'OK. And now for the good news, Sam, which comes directly from my wife, out of Jessica Hamilton at the local Acme.'

After he finished giving him Sally's information, Dawson leaned back in his chair and just stared.

'You're kidding,' he said.

'That's just what I said, Sam.'

'Jesus Christ,' continued Dawson.

'That's just what I said, Sam. By the way, do you think it's all true?'

'Dawson nodded thoughtfully. 'Hell, yes. That's the one thing I've learned about serious gossip. It's almost always true.'

'Well, I'm acting on that, too,' said Constanza. 'I've set up a talk with Beecham over at the University for four o'clock. Even if it's not true, it's logical for me to talk to him early on. Incidentally, we'll want to talk to the girl's parents soon. About any letters she may have written, things she may have told them, stuff like that, right?'

'Right,' said Dawson. 'Turns out they live quite near here, in Makefield County. Quietly rich. Both are lawyers, corporate law types, working in Philadelphia. Waterston's already phoned them, and is going for them in his car. They should be here by early this evening. Staying at the Inn.'

Constanza nodded and began idly collecting his papers and putting them into his bag. He seemed preoccupied. He slowly zipped the bag up and slung it over his shoulder, but made no move to rise. He lowered his head, removed a thread from his trousers, rubbed his cheek and began to carefully study the tips of his shoes. Dawson looked at him and waited quietly.

'Uh, listen, Sam. You know, I've never done anything like this before. You're, uh, going to have to stick your hand in every once in a while. Get the water's temperature, see how it's flowing, where the ripples are going. Know what I mean? I mean, somebody killed that poor kid. Personally stuck a knife into her throat. From the looks of things, it was a personal, vicious thing to do. I haven't...I don't have...'

Dawson leaned forward and was careful not to sound either sarcastic or patronizing. 'You'll do fine, Phil. Just fine. Look, treat it like a puzzle. Most of what you'll be doing initially are all indicated things. You collect your pieces. Your hard information, times, alibis, prints. Your soft information, motive, character, personality. I'm assuming nobody comes forward to make your life easier, like with a confession. So you've got to go out and do it, just like you're doing. This isn't robbery or drugs or speeding on a state highway. This is some basically anomalous person-to-person human conduct stemming from some human trait in the extreme, like jealousy, love, rejection, things like that. Right up your alley. You keep your eyes open, you keep your mind open. You use your local knowledge, of which you have a lot. At first you keep yourself out of it because you don't yet want your own colouration. After a while you'll see some shape. Sometimes even the absence of shape is a shape. Then you might *want* your colouration. The hardest part, Phil, the hardest part is knowing when to listen to your intuition and your feel, and when not to. And nobody can give you any help on that score. We'll talk a lot. Even when you don't think there's anything to say we'll talk because you'd be amazed at how saying something out loud can sometimes put an entirely different cast on it.'

Dawson leaned back on his chair but didn't change the matter-of-factness of his tone. 'And one more thing, Phil: it's good to be polite, but not too polite. Don't take any shit from anyone. They try to do that a lot in this town, especially over at the University, and especially the insecure ones in the Social Sciences and the Arts where measures of concrete achievement are not so easy to come by. From the lowest secretary level all the way up to the chaired professor, position, hierarchy, pecking

order, who ranks whom, well, it's the only thing
they've got that gives them a sense of themselves.
I give shit, therefore I am. Know what I mean? Of
course you know what I mean.'

Dawson stopped. Constanza sat motionless for a
few seconds, then nodded once and rose to go.
Dawson's eyes changed and his voice lightened.
'Good-looking girl, that Twelvetrees.'

'Sure is,' said Constanza.

'Next time you interrogate her, you can let me
know.'

'Next time, Chief, you can have her all to yourself. And thanks for the talk. That was good.'

'Oh, Christ,' said Dawson, 'I almost forgot. There'll be a press conference over at the Inn at six
o'clock. Colonial Room. For any reporters who
show up a little early. Please be there. It'll be you,
me, Waterston and one of his security people.
Same for tomorrow, only tomorrow'll probably be
more full-blown. They'll all be here by then, and
will have had a day to get their bearings and a little
of the lie of the land. After that, we'll see. At these
sessions I'll handle all the police questions, and
you will be back-up. Answer only when I ask you.
The party line will be that the investigation is ongoing and that there is nothing to report. If they
catch you alone, and they will, even if they have
to camp outside your door, and try to pump, and
they will, just repeat the party line. But always
polite, OK? If we're lucky and things are quiet
they should begin to dribble away after two or

three days. A town like this doesn't hold too much attraction for big city reporters. It's one of the few times when lack of a really good restaurant will work in our favour.'

Constanza nodded. 'Fine, Sam. All understood. How about the *Chronicle?*'

'Good question. Same with the *Chronicle.* Except I've already spoken to Charlie Harris, and there are a couple of unofficial things we've worked out. You don't want to know about that, though.'

I'll bet I don't, thought Constanza as he left.

On his way out, he stopped at Mary Underwood's desk. 'I guess we're going to be pretty busy around here for a while, Mary.'

'Oh, we'll do all right, Phil,' she said. She suddenly leaned forward and lowered her voice. 'Listen, you're going to be the main investigator, right? Well, you know what I just heard? I heard that the head of the Art Department—a Professor Beecham?—has been shacking up with that poor girl, and that *she's* been seen over at McCardle's with…'

# EIGHT

CONSTANZA ENTERED the library and, after the heat of the muggy June afternoon, welcomed the coolness of its palazzo-like main lobby. It occurred to him that until this morning he hadn't been in this library for a very long while. When he had first received his appointment as a Police Officer and became a Township Official, he had been given a yearly access card to the Tavistock Library but had renewed it only twice. He shook his head and thought: Christ, the way things slide. Well, two kids, a new household, a new job, could do that.

He stood for a moment and looked around at what appeared to be a typical library scene, and smiled softly to himself as pleasant memories rippled through him. Constanza had always felt comfortable in libraries. He had found them psychologically warm, cosy places. For some reason people were friendly and considerate in libraries. There seemed to be very little harshness about, and even the sounds—the rustle of turning pages, the muted footfalls, the polite whispers—were soft and agreeable. And being surrounded by so much accessible knowledge had been somehow soothing to him. Hell, he suddenly recalled, it was even more than that; it had actually affected him physically, used to relax shoulder and neck muscles, make his breathing freer and less constricted.

From where he was standing in the lobby he could see the principal reading-room, with its banks of card catalogues in their burnished old-wood housings, and the rows of computer screens with their keyboards ready to call up God knows what information. The area was well-populated at this time of day and the mental activity in the air was palpable, almost audible. He surely missed it from his student days. When all this was over, he would have to make a point of renewing his card and start going to the library again, if only for a pleasure that had no equivalent.

But not today.

As he left the lobby and started towards the access office, he noticed isolated signs that things were, in fact, not quite normal. Here and there, in groups of from three to five, students with serious faces and lowered heads stood around whispering. Other students with notebooks and pencils in their hands stopped to listen. Constanza, walking by some of these groups, could hear hushed phrases of... 'yeah, on D-level...in the throat...God, right in the carrel?...roped off with police tape...around eleven, they say...' He wondered if there were going to be as much studying tonight in the library as there usually was, especially in the underground levels. Probably not. Certainly not.

Once in the office, he confirmed from George

Li (who introduced himself as Head of Access, a title that struck Constanza as vaguely salacious) that yes, indeed, you needed either a Photo ID or a stamped and signed temporary access card to get you past the entrance guard, at least up to ten o'clock when the library closed. But Constanza also learned something that he did not know, that cards issued to faculty and students with study carrels had a magnetic strip that enabled them to open one of the side doors even when the library was closed.

'It wasn't always like this, you know,' said George Li. 'Up to about five years ago every adult resident of Kingsford County had access to the library, and there were no guards. But the thefts mounted, you see, and finally someone determined that in one year alone over $30,000 worth of books had disappeared. And even that, by itself, would probably not have been sufficient, except that Dr Thorndyke, the Library's head, discovered one Saturday that thirty-eight per cent of the occupants of the main reading-room were outsiders, and immediately after that the Library Committee voted to restrict access. I mean, losing a lot of money was one thing, Sergeant Constanza, but such flagrant abuse of ''their'' library facilities by outsiders was just too much. And even then it wasn't over because the President had to endorse the decision and Charles Harris over at the *Chronicle* wrote a really blistering series of editorials about how the University was normally bound to share itself with the community within which it functioned and flourished. But in the end, the President had to side with his Library Committee, of course, so now outsider admittance cards cost five hundred dollars and they're almost all held by nearby corporations…'

Constanza had begun edging towards the door, but his experience both as a State Trooper and as a detective on Kingsford's police force told him that once a 'talker' got up this much momentum, stronger action would be necessary to break him off.

He held up a hand. 'Listen,' he interrupted. 'Thanks very much, Mr Li, but I really have to meet someone. Let me catch you up on this when I have more time. Meanwhile thanks very much for the pass.'

Constanza left the office, showed the pass to the entrance guard as he went through a turnstile, and took the stairs down to D-level. The library smell was strong here, a combination of paper, undisturbed dust and floor wax. The only light came from fluorescent light fixtures recessed into the ceiling, and Constanza decided that at two o'clock in the morning this place could be downright spooky. He quickly located Hilda Robertson's carrel from a map George Li had given him and found to his relief that the entire corridor had been roped off with yellow police-line tape and, in addition, had a University security guard stationed at one end. Constanza knew the guard as Eddie, a retired plumber who drove in from Trenton every day.

Almost all the security and maintenance people lived outside Kingsford since typical housing costs were simply beyond their means, and there was a three-year waiting list for the affordable housing units just off the shopping centre.

'Just want to look around, Eddie, OK?'

'Sure, Sergeant Constanza. Everything's pretty much the same as this morning.'

Constanza paused. 'Pretty much?'

'Well, George Talliaferro and his crew came back and dusted some more for prints, and a couple of guys came and waxed the floor. Apart from that, everything's exactly the same, I think. You're the first guy to come around since then. Besides some rubber-necking students, of course.'

'Any of them give you any trouble?'

'Nah. Most of them looked a little scared, as a matter of fact. Shame about the girl, though. Anything happening yet?'

'No. Not a clue.' He didn't smile at the phrase, not even to himself.

Constanza walked slowly to the carrel and again looked inside. This time it was dark and there was no dead girl in it. He slipped on a pair of polyester laboratory gloves and flicked the light switch. Books, a loose-leaf notebook, papers, a yellow legal pad, pencils were all neatly arranged on surfaces. The writing on the pad had stopped in mid-sentence with no tailing scrawl of surprise or violence. There were three books, all open, all having the word Caravaggio in the title, and all stamped 'Kingsford University Library' on the spine. One was blood-smeared. The notebook contained reprints of papers in Spanish apparently presented at some conference in Toledo and had the name 'Caravaggio' liberally sprinkled throughout the text. The loose papers seemed to contain isolated paragraphs with references to journals scribbled beneath them. Constanza took a small notepad and pencil from his shoulder-bag and copied down the titles and authors of the books.

Then for a while he just stood there and looked at the scene, as though by just looking long enough and intently enough he could get some picture of the man (person) who had shown up at Hilda Robertson's elbow, had not surprised her, and then killed her. But all he could come up with was a blank-faced library user, with no suggestion as to height, age, gender, anything helpful. He looked around again at the objects in the carrel, trying to imagine connections from them to some one individual, but all that got him was a vision of Hilda Robertson writing a report.

Think of it as a puzzle, Dawson had said.

He scribbled again in his notepad. Fingerprints, shoeprints, more than one blood type, material under fingernails, guards' rounds, did guard know she was there.

He left the carrel, said 'Thanks' to Eddie, and walked slowly up the stairs back to the main reading-room on the ground floor. He sat down at the clear end of one of the fifteen long communal tables in the centre of the cavernous room, each designed to accommodate up to twenty students. It was three o'clock and the June heat from outside had begun to reach even here. He took off his sweater, tied its sleeves around his waist, leaned over his notepad and promptly became indistinguishable from everyone else. He settled in and looked around. The students were sitting, as though by unwritten agreement, in alternate chairs along the tables, each surrounded by semi-circular arrangements of books, papers, notebooks, pencils and occasionally Kleenex boxes; and although their clothes, colour and faces were different, and they were sprawled in different postures, there was clearly something homogeneous about them. They were all doing the same thing.

After a half-hour of going over his notepad and what he knew so far, Constanza saw nothing to point him in any clear direction. Well, probably too early, he reasoned. After all, less than a day. Patience. The lab work wouldn't even be in until tomorrow. No, not tomorrow, he decided, as he made a final note to ask the lab crew to work straight through for this. That way, he could probably get some answers this evening.

He took a larger notebook out of his shoulder-bag and, starting on a fresh page, rewrote his notes into a neater, more organized format. Then he jotted down some questions for Professor Beecham to make sure he would cover them, and, on a separate sheet of paper, made a list of people he would want to see next: Hilda Robertson's other boy-friend, members of the Art Department who might have been passed over for promotion because of Hilda Robertson's appointment, Bernie McCardle. Then he mentally cursed himself and inserted 'Mrs Beecham' at the head of the list. Christ, he thought, what an omission.

It was a little past three-thirty, and Constanza began gathering his papers together. He put them into his bag and started out. He passed through the exit turnstile, holding the bag open for inspection by the guard, and as he was zipping it up and heading for the exit his eyes strayed to the circulation desk. He frowned in thought and then stopped. Two students bumped into him, one mumbling 'Sorry,' the other saying 'Hey, man.' But Constanza remained frozen as some vague notion first stirred, then evolved in a series of steps that had nothing to do with conscious will, and finally coalesced into a full-blown, gloriously pertinent idea.

He turned on his heel and strode to the circulation desk, confronting a skinny red-haired boy in a denim shirt and beltless khaki pants. 'Excuse me, is there someone in charge here that I could speak with, please?'

'Well, there's Mrs Scully, the Desk Supervisor, but we aren't supposed to bother her except for really important or unusual—'

'Right,' interrupted Constanza. 'Please tell her that this is really important and unusual and that I would like to see her.'

The boy started to say something to him, thought better of it and said, 'OK. Wait just a minute.'

He disappeared into a back room and returned a half-minute later with a thick-waisted fiftyish woman in oversized tortoiseshell eyeglasses, hair that was beginning to straggle and make-up that was beginning to streak. She wore dangling turquoise earrings. She marched straight to the counter, looked levelly at Constanza and said, 'Well, young man, I'm Mrs Scully and would you please tell me what is so important and unusual.' She made no attempt to temper her tone of voice.

Constanza leaned forward and said, 'Mrs Scully, could we talk in your office, please?'

'Not until you tell me what about, young man. I'm quite busy, so why don't you just state your business.'

Constanza supposed that, dressed as he was, he could easily pass for an older grad student, and, of course, Mrs Scully might just be having a bad day; nevertheless she was beginning to rankle. 'Well, Mrs Scully, I'm Detective-Sergeant Constanza investigating the murder of Hilda Robertson and I have a few questions I'd like to ask you.'

While not shouting, he had not spoken particularly softly either, and two of the clerks stopped what they had been doing, turned to him and unashamedly gaped. The librarian herself blinked twice, then opened her mouth and closed it. Her colour faded. Constanza judged it highly unlikely that a police officer had ever spoken to her like this before.

She cleared her throat, looked around once, and said, 'Please come with me.' She lifted a hinged flap in the counter to let him through and led him down a narrow corridor into a windowless, claustrophobic office that seemed to have been constructed in very much of a hurry.

She cleared her throat again. 'Please sit down, Mr Constanza. And how may I help you?' She remained pale.

Constanza tried to make his voice friendly, and even smiled a little. 'Please relax, Mrs Scully. I'd just like to get some information about library operations. Tell me, if I gave you the names of some books, could you tell me who were the last half-dozen or so people who had checked them out?'

'Yes, of course,' she said, still in a subdued voice. 'We would have all that in our storage file.' She motioned not to the two old filing cabinets against a wall, but rather to a computer perched on a small table at the side of her desk.

Constanza slid across the sheet of paper with the titles of the three Caravaggio books in Hilda Robertson's carrel. 'Please give me the names of the last, oh, five people who checked these books out. I'll be glad to wait.'

'Certainly,' said the librarian, and, turning to the computer, began tapping on the keyboard. Soon, lines of green type began appearing on the monitor screen. 'Would you like a print-out?' she asked.

'That would be just fine, if you wouldn't mind.'

More green lines appeared, and occasionally the keyboard tapping would stop and from the floor underneath the computer table the sound of a printer at work would be heard. Constanza forced himself to wait patiently. After a while, Mrs Scully stooped down and tore off a sheet of computer paper from a large roll and passed it over.

'Here, under each of the titles, are the names of the people you wanted plus the dates during which the books were checked out to them. Is that what you wanted?'

'Exactly right, Mrs Scully.' His voice trailed off with preoccupation as he pored quickly over the information. 'Exactly right,' he said again, almost under his breath.

Suddenly, he jumped up. 'Goddamn!' he said. 'Goddamn!'

The librarian recoiled and actually brought her hands to her throat. But Constanza was oblivious of everything except what was there in front of him. 'Of course,' he whispered to the paper in his hand. 'Of course.'

He turned to the librarian. 'Mrs Scully, you've been very helpful, really very helpful. Thank you very much.'

He looked at his watch. Ten minutes to four. Time to get to Professor Beecham's.

He hardly noticed the bicycle ride over to the Arts building as he chewed, swallowed and digested the fact that all three of the Caravaggio books in Hilda Robertson's carrel had been checked out to the same person at various times, and had been returned the day before the murder, and all, of course, had been checked out by Hilda Robertson on the day she was killed.

# NINE

PROFESSOR STANLEY BEECHAM had wanted to see
Constanza at his flat, but Constanza had insisted
on his campus office. This was mostly for his, Constanza's, benefit. He was already convinced that
the murder, and its solution, was a University affair
and he wanted to conduct his investigation as much
as possible within the physical—and psychological—confines of the University.

The building housing the Art Department was
sufficiently old so that its ground-floor offices had,
according to the architectural style of its day, unusually high ceilings. Professor Beecham, the Department head, had the best of these. A frowning
departmental secretary who seemed to radiate officious protectiveness ushered Constanza into an
office considerably larger than Sam Dawson's.
Books and manuscripts were everywhere, on sol-
idly packed shelves that circled the walls and ran
to the ceiling, on the ledge of a double-wide bay
window, on chairs scattered about, even stacked on
the floor in various corners. The room literally
smelled, not unpleasantly, of old and new paper.
There were a desk and a table in the room, both
almost completely clear, so situated that a large

swivel chair could rotate on its base from one to the other and allow its occupant to work conveniently on either surface.

Professor Beecham smiled and got up smoothly to shake Constanza's hand. He was a full three inches taller than Constanza's five feet-ten and with just as flat a stomach. He had a craggily lined face highlighted by energetic blue eyes and steel-grey hair cut with some care to medium short length. His speech was thoughtfully modulated and delivered in the soft but firm bass tones that indicate familiarity with the exercise of power. He would make, thought Constanza, a first-rate father-figure with sexual advantages for a lot of girls, and even as he took his hand he was forming a dislike for him.

Beecham motioned Constanza to the only chair with no books on it and said, 'You're right on time, Sergeant Constanza. I presume you're here about the Robertson girl's death, is that right?'

'Yes, it is, Professor Beecham.' He took the tape-recorder out of his bag and clicked it on. He thought he might as well start right in. 'Sir, what was your relationship with Miss Robertson?'

Beecham paused a moment, then said, 'Well, why don't you tell me what you know of it and I'll fill in what's missing or what's wrong.'

Constanza couldn't help smiling, because it was just what he needed to put his frame of mind into the more assertive mode that he was groping for. 'No, Professor Beecham, it doesn't work that way.

I'm investigating a murder and I have some questions for you and you answer them as you may see fit.'

Beecham paused again, this time a bit longer. 'I see.' He smiled. Then: 'Tell me, Sergeant Constanza, should I have a lawyer present?'

Constanza did not smile back. 'We can do this in two ways, Professor. I can obtain a warrant, place you under arrest as a material witness, read you your rights and question you in the interrogation room at the police station. In which case you would certainly want a lawyer present. Or we can chat unofficially in which you simply act cooperatively and try to contribute to the investigation, in which case neither a warrant nor a lawyer is really necessary. But it's your choice. Just for the record, you are at this time considered neither more nor less a suspect than any one else.'

Beecham assumed a serious mien and said, 'Well, all right, why don't we just start here, then. To answer your first question, yes, I have been seeing Miss Robertson.'

'Have you been having an affair with her, that is, sleeping with her on a more or less periodic basis either at your apartment or hers?'

'Yes, I have.' Beecham's tone was curt but Constanza didn't mind at all.

'And about how long has this been going on?'

'Oh, about six months, I should think.'

'So that would make it about the time you and

Mrs Beecham separated and Miss Robertson received her appointment as Assistant Professor.'

Beecham didn't miss a beat. 'Yes, about that time. But for the record that appointment was made solely on scholastic merit and you would be wrong to think otherwise. Hilda Robertson was, in my judgement, an exceptionally gifted person and had the makings of a first-rate art historian. She was well into her doctoral thesis and I saw the appointment as ultimately serving the best interests of the Department and the University. An available hiring slot was open in the department and I chose to fill it. The appointment, by the way, was not yet on to a tenure track.'

'I see. And what does such a tenure track involve, Professor?'

'Usually a doctorate and an appointment as, or promotion to, Associate Professor.'

'When she would have gotten her doctorate, would such a promotion have been in the offing?'

'*If* she got her doctorate. That would be subject to thesis acceptance and committee approval. And we do have high standards here.'

'But say she did get it. Could promotion to associate professor be made solely by you?'

'Yes, it could. But anything further, say the actual granting of tenure, could follow only by committee action. Incidentally, Hilda—Miss Robertson—knew all this, of course.'

'I see. Does a tenure track appointment customarily result in the granting of tenure, Professor? Is it all more or less automatic?'

'Not at all, Sergeant, at least not at Kingsford. Usually, in fairness to all parties, a decision is made after three years, and as a rule a significant number of applicants are not approved.'

'Tell me, Professor Beecham, can the granting or withholding of tenure be as delicate, political, capricious, and ruthless a process as the rumours have it?'

Now Beecham did miss a beat. He paused but did not alter his facial expression as he said, 'Sergeant Constanza, you have no idea. But a discussion of that is not why we are here, is it?'

'No, that's right. Tell me, were you her thesis adviser?'

'Yes, and chairman of her doctoral committee.'

'And what was her thesis topic, please?'

'The role of secular and ecclesiastical patronage in Post-Renaissance art. And is that all really relevant?'

'Yes, sir, please bear with me. Would you say that Caravaggio was a painter who would be included in such a thesis?'

'Oh, he would be—would have to be—a prime figure. Central, you might say. You could almost make such a study just of him alone.'

'So that you would expect that somewhere along the line Hilda Robertson would be interested in him.'

There was a respectful knock at the door and

without an answer the secretary entered, put a cup of coffee on the table at Beecham's elbow and left. On her way out, she glanced sideways at Constanza, still frowning. There were two cookies on the saucer along with three lumps of sugar wrapped in paper. Constanza noted that there already was cream in the coffee. Beecham dropped two of the lumps into the coffee and began nibbling at a cookie.

'As a matter of fact,' he said, 'she was just getting into Caravaggio. It was the last major section of her thesis and he was to be treated as archetypal and one of the strongest figures of the period.'

Constanza reached into his bag, brought out his sheet of notes and read to him the book titles he had written down.

Beecham nodded several times and said, 'Yes, I know the books well. They are definitive and almost seminal to what we are talking about. May I ask why these particular books?'

'Sure. They were the ones Miss Robertson was working from in her carrel when she was murdered.' Constanza watched Beecham for his reaction, but all he did was put the last of the second cookie into his mouth, drink some of the coffee and say, 'Right. As a matter of fact, Sergeant, Miss Robertson was waiting for those very books to be returned. She was most anxious to get at them.'

See how cooperative I am being, he could have added.

Constanza was having a hard time trying to

gauge Beecham. After all, he might have made love to her less than forty-eight hours ago and now he was discussing her murder with the equanimity of a man who was contentedly having his afternoon coffee. Constanza would have loved to break through his veneer of dispassion, or at least to determine if it were more than just veneer, but didn't know how.

'I have just one more question, Professor Beecham. Can you account for your whereabouts last night between the hours of, say, eleven p.m. and three a.m.?'

Beecham's smile was broad and, Constanza grudgingly admitted to himself, very attractive. 'Why, I certainly can, Sergeant. I was at my estranged wife's last night. Showed up around eleven, left around seven-thirty. Part of our separation agreement is that she gets to live in the house and I and my clothes move out, all provided she lets me stay overnight and use it for University business occasionally. Sometimes it's convenient for me. And besides, my lawyer says that it may have legal significance down the road in case we have to dicker over who gets the house in possible divorce proceedings.'

'Does Mrs Beecham know that?'

'I don't know, Sergeant. That's her lookout, not mine.'

'Right,' said Constanza, and began to gather his things. When he had started his questioning he had not yet decided whether to disclose by his questions all the information he possessed, such as Hilda Robertson's other boyfriend. He was still undecided but finally ruled it out, if only temporarily. He felt that this would not be the last time he would be questioning Beecham and when he next saw him and did bring up other matters he preferred to have more information under his belt.

He rose. 'Oh, one final thing. If you plan on leaving Kingsford, even for an overnight or two, please let me know.'

'Am I a suspect, Sergeant Constanza?'

'Right now there are no suspects, Professor Beecham. But you are a very material part of our investigation. Surely that's fair to say.'

Beecham nodded, Constanza nodded back and left.

As he went through the anteroom the secretary raised her head from her typewriter and again glared at him accusingly. It nettled him. The whole interview nettled him. He felt that Beecham had gotten the better of him, had actually controlled the tone and shape of the interview. He felt he should have done a better job at discomforting Beecham, at putting him off balance. He felt he should have prepared a little more, worked out his series of questions a little more thoroughly. What he, Constanza, did not know was that compared with what Beecham typically had to handle at some of his meetings with the Dean of Faculty on curriculum, or with the other Department heads on the disposition of the annual budget, an interrogation like this was child's play.

He turned to the secretary. 'Excuse me, ma'am. May I...' He stopped. 'Look, I want to dial directly to one of the dorm rooms. Can I use that phone in the corner for that?'

She compressed her lips. Constanza remained immobile and continued to look directly at her with an unblinking impassivity. After a few moments she nodded and said, 'Yes.'

He dialled Leonard Friedman's room number and after the second ring a voice with the unmistakable swagger of the city streets said, 'Yeah?'

'Mr Leonard Friedman.'

'Yes, this is he.'

Constanza couldn't help smiling at the jarring note of fastidious grammar. 'My name is Constanza, Sergeant Philip Constanza, of the Kingsford Police Department. I'm investigating the murder of Hilda Robertson and I'd like to talk to you privately for just a few minutes. It would be appreciated.'

Constanza waited patiently for all this to be digested. He guessed it would take about five seconds and it did.

Then, 'Really?'

'Yes, really, Mr Friedman.'

'OK. Where'd you like to do that?'

'How about the access office in the main lobby of Tavistock Library. Do you know where that is?'

'Sure, I'll be there in five minutes, OK?'

'OK.' Too late Constanza realized he hadn't asked for a description of Leonard Friedman. Christ, he couldn't even tell from the voice if he were white or black. And nowadays you couldn't be sure even with a name like Friedman.

# TEN

IT WAS TEN MINUTES past six and Sam Dawson
reluctantly agreed with Gerald Waterston that they
should start without Sergeant Constanza. The fifteen chairs were all filled, a half-dozen standees
lounged against the walls, and the audience had
become considerably more restive during the last
couple of minutes. Dawson's estimate of less than
fifteen reporters from newspapers was accurate
enough but what he had forgotten was Television
news teams from *Action News* in Philadelphia and
*Live at Five* from New York that included video
cameramen and lighting technicians. Dawson
cursed himself for his oversight and hoped that this
was not an omen of things to come. In any event,
there was damned little information to pass on to
them and both Dawson and Waterston felt that the
sooner this first meeting was over, the better.

Dawson and Hal Jamison, his college-days
buddy from the *Baltimore Sun,* had talked privately
over a quick sandwich in Dawson's office, during
which time Jamison convinced Dawson that the reporters were not going to be controlled as easily
as Dawson had thought, but would have to be allowed some time for independent investigation. A

full-frontal murder at a place like Kingsford mer-
ited attention—at least a couple of articles, and
maybe even a feature, from any worthwhile reporter. When asked how much attention, Jamison
replied that if no juicy developments surfaced, the
reporters might begin to get tired of Kingsford in
a couple of days. Also their papers might recall
them. Dawson thanked him and said he would try
to give him an inside track on things when results
began to come in. On his way out of the office, he
learned from Mary Underwood that no, Constanza
had not phoned in, nor had he phoned his wife all
afternoon.

The press conference did not go well, but was
no disaster either. Waterston had changed his suit
to a much darker shade of grey. Both Dawson and
George Pelletieri, the portly, shrewd-eyed Chief of
University Security, were in uniform. To everyone's relief Constanza showed up at the last minute, breathing hard.

The room itself was pretty bad. The ceiling
seemed at least six inches lower than the typical
ceiling. The paint on the back wall had begun to
peel. The overhead fluorescent lights looked dingy
and seemed to throw pallor rather than light, and
when the television lights came on, the room, in
its garish brightness, somehow became even more
depressing. The chairs were wooden-slatted rather
than the moulded plastic often seen in hotel meet-
ing-rooms. There was indeed only one water-
cooler flanked by a column of those cone-shaped

paper cups Dawson so vehemently detested. He wondered if he had overdone the poor room bit but finally decided the hell with it, he had enough troubles to worry about, the principal one being that he had no idea how Constanza was going to perform in this situation without any briefing or rehearsal.

Waterston spoke first, mouthing for the most part appropriate platitudes with appropriate feelings of tragedy, shock and outrage.

But towards the end of the delivery he began to deviate from the smoothness of prepared text and started to speak haltingly and with obvious extemporization. His emotion seemed to become more heartfelt. He spoke of a brutal murder of a promising young member of the University community. Nothing even remotely like it had ever occurred before at Kingsford and it would leave its mark forever. It had happened on his, Waterston's, watch and he felt somehow vaguely responsible. It was stupid, he supposed, but that was the way he felt. This was not just an abstraction, he went on, but a concrete and permanent part of Kingsford's history. 'Do not misunderstand me,' he continued in a suddenly stronger voice, 'I am not speaking of a girl's death, now. That tragedy is of an incomparable dimension, one indeed that only parents and loving friends can truly comprehend. But this murder, this abomination, did not happen in a subway in New York or in a dark alley in Detroit. It happened here in this privileged place for the mind,

situated in a town of bright sunshine and flowering
trees. Like many other human events, I suppose, it
should not have happened, was not supposed to
happen. It is a gross, gross injustice, a monstrous
aberration in what we try to do here and it must
now be addressed so that the balance can be re-
stored.' He paused then, dimly aware that somehow, something had gone unexpectedly off the
plan. He was not supposed to be saying these
things at this time. He was not supposed to be feeling this way. He had taken a liberty in this carefully structured event and indulged his sense of
indignation.

His right hand had become clenched without his
realizing it, and now he looked down at it,
frowned, and slowly unclenched it. He seemed at
a loss as to what exactly to say or do next.

For a few moments no one spoke or moved, although the soundless television cameras continued
turning. Several of the audience shifted about in
their seats, sensing that they had witnessed an unexpected intimacy. Sam Dawson was the one who
broke the spell. He rose, said softly, 'Thank you,
Professor Waterston,' and beckoned him to a chair.
Then he turned and addressed the reporters in a
businesslike tone, describing Kingsford's police resources, how the investigation was being set up,
their access to high-tech forensics in New York
and Philadelphia if that became necessary. He then
introduced Pelletieri and Constanza and said that
they would fill in the details of how the body was

found and the current state of the investigation—which, it must be realized, was just starting.

One of the things Dawson had earlier told both Waterston and Pelletieri was to be quite free with any detail a good reporter would be able to find out anyhow for himself. Thus, Pelletieri gave Janet Twelvetrees's story in full detail, then described the condition of the carrel down to its lack of disarray and even included the books that Constanza had noted. He gave the list of security guards on patrol at the approximate time of the killing. Pelletieri finished by saying that none of the guards on patrol duty had reported either seeing or hearing anything unusual. He did not mention the library access system, the need for Photo IDs, the electronically accessible side door, or the fact that Twelvetrees had been living in the library for over a month.

Dawson then rose, but before he could say anything, one of the reporters shouted out, 'Chief, we gonna get a chance to ask any questions?'

'Of course,' answered Dawson. 'I just thought it would be better if we finished first so that you people would have the whole picture of what was going on. There'll be unlimited questions after we're done, if that's OK with you.' There was no answer from the audience, which Dawson's experience told him was the closest he was going to get to acquiescence from a roomful of reporters. Dawson then went on to introduce Detective-Sergeant Philip Constanza 'in charge of the investigation and reporting to me', then sat down and mentally crossed his fingers.

But he needn't have worried. Constanza simply said that the investigation was just getting started, that he had spoken to Miss Twelvetrees and Professor Beecham, the Art Department head, and that forensics had spent the whole morning going over the scene of the murder and he would begin to get some of their reports later on this evening, although he could say even now that there were no fingerprints on the murder weapon. He hoped he could have considerably more for them tomorrow evening. He spoke smoothly and quietly and Dawson made a note to himself to compliment him on his delivery. In fact, thought Dawson, this whole thing was beginning to sound, and perhaps too much, like some well-oiled corporate presentation.

'Questions, anyone?' said Dawson.

The very first question, from the *New York Post* man surprisingly well-dressed in lightweight olive sharkskin and coordinated striped tie, told everyone that it was not going to be all that easy. 'Chief, please forgive me, but what I'd like to know is what exactly is it you're trying to hide? Just what are you wanting to keep from us in this overarranged meeting? Look, was this girl single, married, engaged, screwing around? Who walks around in a library at midnight? Who could be jealous of her? Is her correspondence being examined? Her phone calls? For Chrissake, Chief, give us a break. If you don't let us have any more than this,

I for one am going to start speculating and you might not like what I often speculate about.'

So much for trying to control the big-city press.

Dawson rose, knowing that something had to be said, and fast, that would answer that and put it to bed and it was just as well sooner than later. 'Yeah, well, I'll tell you, sir. What we're trying to hide from you is the fact that we don't have a clue as to what went on down here. Literally. Yes, we're pushing all that stuff you mentioned but nothing has shown up yet. Yes, jealousy is as good a motive as any, but what kind and by whom is something you can conjecture on as well as we. Hell, this is the first day. There's a little shock around, you know? The legwork is just starting and by a lot more people than what's up here and by tomorrow night there'll be a lot more that's come in.' He paused. 'And listen, just one more thing while we're on it. We're gonna be as candid as we can with you guys, but to tell you the truth, if we got something going and making it public might screw it up, well, we're just not gonna give it to you. Now, you may not like that and I know you can write what you damn like but that's the way it's going to be and, well, I hope you understand our viewpoint on this. Anything more detailed than that, you ask Constanza or Pelletieri here, OK?'

He sat down, more or less satisfied with himself. Not only had he stood up well to the first attempt at intimidation, but he felt he had struck the balanced note of openness and autonomy he had wanted. And he had also managed to give the message to his people up here with him.

The questions started immediately, and almost all of them were directed at Constanza.

Nothing in Constanza's experience had prepared him for this. On his Turnpike duty there had been mostly speeding and reckless driving. Occasionally, there was a quarrel between the parties of an accident. On a handful of occasions there had been a drug search triggered by a tip from an informer. But that was about it. His work in Kingsford was connected mostly with burglary, disturbing the peace and a few cases of sexual assault. Answering a barrage of questions from a roomful of reporters was completely new to him, and he almost instantly decided that temporary evasion was the better part of candour.

Taking his cue from Dawson, Constanza deflected most of the questions on the grounds of lack of knowledge, or postponed them until the next session tomorrow. There were only two difficult moments. The man from the *New York Times*, pudgy, with thin hair and a strong Boston accent, asked outright if anyone could get into the library at any hour. Constanza cleared his throat to mask a couple of seconds' thought and then decided that you couldn't hide such knowledge forever and so described in detail the access procedures, finishing with the thought that yes, that should ordinarily limit the circle of possible killers, and their investigation was certainly reflecting that although there was still nothing that had turned up. The other bad moment came when one of the television reporters asked if any known romantic involvements had come to light yet, and Constanza decided simply to lie. It could always be corrected later after 'more information' had turned up and Constanza just didn't know what kind of rat's nest telling the truth might open up. And, besides, he strongly suspected he would not handle it well.

The last words were spoken by Dawson. He said that the parents of the girl did not want to talk to any reporters, and that the funeral would be held privately near their home. As for the rest, the addresses and phone numbers of the principals were all in the phone book.

Dawson had gauged one thing correctly, though. As the meeting was breaking up several reporters asked what were some good restaurants in Kingsford, and Dawson took private pleasure in saying that, honestly, there simply weren't any. He said that the hotel would do as well as any place in town, and that there was a Chinese restaurant around the corner on Delaware Avenue.

# ELEVEN

'SORRY I WAS LATE but I just couldn't break off.
Sam, I was mining pure gold.' Constanza was gesticulating and talking with an excitement completely at odds with his usual demeanour. 'Listen,
I think I now know how—'

Dawson abruptly cut him off. 'Just a minute,
Phil, OK? Just calm down. And for Chrissake
lower your voice.'

They were standing in a corner of the lobby.
Several of the reporters were still drifting around
talking with each other or reading the Kingsford
Community bulletin board just to the left of the
registration desk. The man from the *New York Post*
was wandering around the rustic-looking lobby and
talking to the *Action News* crew about '...high
class, academic quaint'. Another group of reporters
had gathered around Professor Waterston, who
stood with his hands in his pockets and head
slightly stooped. His posture was most professional, simultaneously indicating close attention to
what was being asked, hearing you out completely
with understanding and patience, and somehow
giving the impression that after you were through
he would have no trouble giving you your answer.

He seemed very much at ease being a centre of attention.

'Come with me a second, Phil,' said Dawson. They headed across the lobby to where Harvey Stanwood was chatting with a tall angular man with sandy hair and a fair complexion. 'Sorry to interrupt, Mr Stanwood, but could you please do me a favour? I was wondering if there might be a small room available for a few minutes where Sergeant Constanza and I could go over some matters in private?'

'Sure, Chief Dawson,' said Stanwood. 'Just go into my office there and ask my secretary for the keys to the Staff Conference room. Tell her I said it was OK. By the way, were the—ah—facilities for your meeting satisfactory?'

'They were just fine, Mr Stanwood,' said Dawson. 'Just fine. Appreciate it very much.'

Constanza and Dawson mouthed polite leave-takings, got the keys from Stanwood's secretary, and after they were ensconced in the Staff meeting-room, Dawson turned to Constanza and said, 'OK, Phil. Now.'

But then he abruptly held up his hand. 'Before you start, though, I just want to tell you that you looked pretty good up there. All things considered, we all did OK. So, what do you know, Phil?'

Constanza leaned forward in his chair. 'I know how the murderer placed Hilda Robertson in the carrel last night at about eleven o'clock.'

Dawson sat up. 'Really?'

'Yes, really.' Constanza then went on to describe his scene with Mrs Scully of the Circulation Department that had led to the fact that all three books that Hilda Robertson had been working on when she was killed—the three books that Beecham had thought were seminal to her work—had all been accumulated by the same person and then returned the day before the killing.

'All he had to do, Sam, was see if the books were still on the shelves, and if they were not, he knew exactly where to find her.'

'If he knew where her study carrel was,' said Dawson.

'There's a public list of assigned study carrels posted in the library,' said Constanza.

Dawson grunted, reached out and said, 'Let me see that read-out, Phil.'

Constanza rummaged in his shoulder-bag and dug out the computer read-out Mrs Scully had given him.

Dawson studied it for a few minutes, then said, 'There's more here than just that, Phil. Look. Look at this. This next-to-last column here shows just what you said. All books returned the same day. Yesterday. But now look at the previous checkout dates. They're all different. That means the guy checked them out over the course of about a month, and each time from a different previous user.'

'Yeah,' said Constanza. 'But I don't get it. What exactly does that mean?'

'It means planning, Phil. Forethought. Lots of forethought. Look, if what you say is true, and the purpose of returning all the books at once was to get Robertson into that study carrel, then the accumulation of these books was, naturally, essential. And getting hold of them over a period of time, waiting for three different people to turn them in, suggests to me some serious intent. This was a long-term plan, Phil.' Dawson paused and looked thoughtful. 'Provided, of course, he was not using them for some legitimate Caravaggio work of his own, right? So, Constanza, your next step is, clearly, to identify all the parties from the card numbers on this read-out.'

Constanza found himself unable to resist it. 'Right, and after you do that, Dawson, this is what you find.' He again rummaged in his bag and then pulled out two more sheets and laid them before Dawson.

Dawson grinned. 'So that's why you were late, right?'

'Right. Now look at this.' They both bent their heads over the papers. 'The three people who had these books prior to the killer's checking them out were all different, just as you say. Two were in Professor Lupescu's class on the something-or-other of Renaissance Art. The third was Lupescu himself. All OK in the sense that having the books is understandable.'

Dawson leaned back in his chair and took a deep breath. 'But now you're going to surprise me about the guy who checked them all out, kept them for a couple of weeks, and then returned them all the day before the murder.'

'Very good, Sam. Really very good. Yes. That man is one Lionel Friedman, grad student in Physics, who remembers once buying a Coke for Hilda Robertson, *and* who also reported a missing or stolen library Photo ID a little over a month ago.'

Sam Dawson half closed his eyes, slid down on his chair, locked his hands behind his neck and gazed at the ceiling. The room became very quiet. Constanza forced himself to remain silent and to make Dawson speak first. For fully thirty seconds the only sound in the room was muted clicks of a large-faced institutional clock mounted high up on the wall.

Dawson finally said, 'You think there's any chance at all that it's going to be this easy?'

Constanza smiled.

'I'm dead serious,' continued Dawson. 'I've never seen anything so damned pat. You've done fine work, Phil. In one day you've turned up a possible murderer with an investigative line that has an almost geometrical neatness. To tell you the truth, I'm a little surprised. Tell me, how do you feel about it all?'

'I don't know, Sam. I didn't expect to have so much, so soon. I only stayed with this guy Friedman long enough to get all this stuff and to establish the fact that his library ID was indeed replaced

by security last month. And then I rushed over
here. Oh, incidentally when you check a book out
at the library, all that's needed is the bar code on
the back of the card, not the photo side, so the
photo never has to be checked against the holder.'

Dawson first nodded, then shook his head. 'I just
don't believe it all. Too good to be true. Just like
you said, solid gold. Tell me, you form any opinion
about this Friedman guy?'

'I'm still in the fact-gathering mode, Sam. Not
ready to put my own slant on things yet. Remember, that's what you said earlier today.'

'Yeah, don't rub it in.' They both sat for a while.
Dawson bent over the read-out sheets again. 'Phil,
what do these asterisks mean?'

Dawson looked at the sheets and shrugged his
shoulders. 'I really don't know, Sam. But I can find
out pretty quickly.' It was too late to get any of
the day staff at the library, but the circulation desk
was, of course, manned until closing time at ten.
After the third try someone told him about the asterisks. He hung up and turned to Dawson. 'Apparently, it means that those books were found in
the book-return drop in the morning. Since the
book drop is cleared at closing time the previous
night, that means that they were returned between
closing time of the previous day and opening time
the next morning.'

Dawson nodded thoughtfully, then shrugged,
drew himself up in his chair and said, 'Well, shit,
we can't just sit here all day. Let's do the indicated

thing and get him in here for questioning. God knows we have enough for that, anyhow. Listen, you mind if we do that together? I can probably do a better job at intimidation than you can.' It was said very matter-of-factly. Constanza didn't for a moment doubt that it was true.

'Absolutely,' he said.

On their way out of the hotel, Dawson stopped to get a candy bar at the newspaper stand and to phone his office. Constanza could see him making notes for a few minutes as he listened, then finally hang up and make another phone call. After the call, he left the phone booth and motioned to Constanza.

'I played back my message machine, and there are a couple of things.' Dawson looked down at his notes. 'Waterston called to say he thought that the press conference was OK but that we should definitely get together before tomorrow night's conference which might well be more difficult. He's probably right. Then Tom Stevens at forensics called to say that he was sorry but nothing showed from the carrel except some smudged prints from the outside door knob. They couldn't do anything with that, so they dismantled the knob and drove the whole thing down to Trenton where they've got some fancy computerized image enhancer apparatus that might yield something. That was smart. Stevens used my name. The guy's name in Trenton is Ritchie DiMarco. I think I know him. Said he might have something by early afternoon.

Stevens's wife is due to go into labour any hour now, so if we've got nothing on tomorrow maybe we could run down there and see what they've got.' Dawson looked up at Constanza. 'But we don't hold our breath on this.' He dropped his eyes back to his notes. 'The most interesting message here is from Professor Stanley Beecham who is having his end-of-term departmental tea at his home—former home—tomorrow afternoon at four-thirty. All the major Department people will be there and in the spirit of helping the investigation we are invited to meet and talk with whomever we want and in any format.' He looked up. 'Well, Sergeant Constanza, and just what do you make of that?'

Constanza smiled. 'Christ, Sam, I don't know.' He shook his head. 'Too damned much happening. Too much being thrown at us for one day. Listen, is it always like this? How was it in Philadelphia when you were there?'

'Well, Philadelphia is a little bigger than Kingsford, you know, and you generally can't pick up the phone and make an appointment with somebody in half an hour and then ride your bike over. No, you're right. This is a lot of stuff for one day. You set something up with this Friedman guy yet?'

'Tentatively at nine o'clock tomorrow morning. I said I'd let him know where at about eight-thirty.'

'OK. Listen, why don't you stop by the office at around eight and we'll map out the day.'

'Right. By the way, do we go to that party at Beecham's, Sam?'

'Wouldn't miss it for the world,' said Dawson.

# TWELVE

SALLY MADE BUCKWHEAT pancakes for breakfast next morning. Real buckwheat flour wasn't available in Kingsford, not even at the local health food store. But the large supermarkets that catered to the black neighbourhoods in and near Trenton carried it routinely, and when Sally heard that Phil was probably going to make a trip to Trenton she said that she would use up the last of her supply ahead of schedule, so would he stop off and get two or three boxes on his way back. Early in their marriage Phil had told her that he liked buckwheat pancakes so much (especially when sandwiched with thinly sliced hickory-smoked ham) that she shouldn't make them more than once or twice a week, and preferably at the weekend. She had asked him if he felt the same way about sex; he had said no, he didn't and she had said that that was the right answer.

A mini weather front had come through from the northwest during the night leaving the morning air light and sparkling, a relief after the sultry haze of the previous few days. After kissing Sally goodbye he went through his ritual of checking his shoul-

der-bag, tyre pressure and helmet, and started out
for the Municipal Building.

The first half-mile of the trip invariably required
the most attentiveness on his part. The roads here
were mostly commercial and were heavily trav-
elled by delivery trucks and morning shoppers
headed for the shopping centre. But once past this
section, the rest of his journey involved a network
of quiet luxury neighbourhoods running around the
rim of Kingsford Township in which lawns and
hedges were professionally cared for and many of
the homes were large enough to house a live-in
servant or two. Here, there was only the occasional
car and Constanza was free to let his mind roam.

There was no getting around it, yesterday had
been a unique day in his life and, on reflection, and
what with the lovely weather, he couldn't help
feeling, well, exultant. And being the person he
was, he began scrutinizing this feeling as he cycled
along, picking at it and questioning it. Constanza
liked to indulge in the examination of human feeling and behaviour—even his own—because he enjoyed peeling back the layers and getting to the
kernel of it. Often, very often, the process defied a
smooth rationality. But in this case his feeling was
easy to diagnose as coming from an exuberance of
spirit that clearly came from doing well at a new
activity. It was well beyond mere contentment; ex-
hilaration was much closer to it. For Constanza, of
course, the next step was suspicion, because one
of the worst sins in his book was smugness. It had

always been a tricky business with him, this balance between warranted self-satisfaction, proper self-abnegation, and a wholesome self-image. And if guilt were thrown in...

He forced his thinking to the day ahead.

So far, the only things scheduled were the interview with Friedman, the trip to the Police Laboratories in Trenton and Beecham's party at four-thirty. Actually, these could well take up most of the day. But Constanza had some more people he wanted to talk to, and as soon as possible. Beecham's wife was one, and Hilda Robertson's other boyfriend, as yet unidentified, was another. And then, there were all the others who knew Hilda Robertson, colleagues, girlfriends, current and former room-mates. Maybe by then he'd have a little better idea of what kind of girl it had been who had gotten murdered. It occurred to him that he had never thought of that, that the kind of girl she had been could have a bearing on finding the killer. But now that it had come to mind it seemed almost obvious.

In fact, he thought to himself as he pedalled along, he had never actually thought of her as a person at all. Maybe just a bit in the carrel yesterday afternoon, but even then it was mostly in connection with a job of work.

She was, of course, more than that. She was a girl working for a graduate degree, just as he himself had once been. She had goals and problems and boyfriends and parents. She wore eyeglasses and ate meals and laughed in the student lounge. And then someone she knew had stuck a knife in her throat and she had bled to death. She had become lifeless. She had changed into a thing without life, just one of several objects in a job-related matter requiring his attention at the moment.

A quiver of low-level nausea rippled through him, and his shoulders twitched. Christ, in all his life, in his three years on the Turnpike and his six here at Kingsford, this was the closest connection to death he had ever known in his line of work. He had never even seen a dead body. Wasn't that an unusual thing for a police officer of nine years to be able to say? Well, maybe for an inner-city cop, for somebody like Sam Dawson, it might be, but apparently for a privileged cop's life in a town like Kingsford, for a life like Philip Constanza's, it needn't be.

He returned to thinking about the murderer, this person who had killed a grad student finishing up a Ph.D. thesis, and found that personalizing the victim was making him think in more personal terms about the killer as well. He seemed less an abstraction, now, and more a particular someone— with a job, a room to sleep in, a car (or a bicycle). He was someone who walked the campus and greeted peers and chatted in doorways. He tried to picture him engaged in these activities, as though that might help identify him. But nothing came of it, no vocation, no age, no shape, not even a hint of a face. And just why the hell should it, he said to himself.

Constanza automatically slipped into a lower gear as his thighs began to feel the upgrade of Stafford Hill, and continued his ruminations. He tried to imagine performing the act of forcing a knife deep into someone's soft-fleshed, living throat and being so personally responsible for ending life. He couldn't. It was, for him, literally unimaginable, an unconscionable act of physical and moral violence. Not only that, but no one he knew could do that. He was sure of it. Yet it might very well turn out to be someone he knew. And if that happened, he wondered, would he ever be able to think of people in exactly the same way as he had all his life?

He turned into Brook Lane for the final run up to the Municipal Building. This was usually the most enjoyable part of the trip, for there actually was a good-sized brook running parallel to the roadway, and it was generally so quiet that you could clearly hear it bubbling along. And on clear days like today the sun slanting through the trees produced a dappling on the road that never failed to lift his spirits. But not this morning. Constanza decided that he had no right to enjoy his cycling on this lovely June morning. Maybe others did, but not him. He had not been serious enough in this matter, he decided. Dawson had been wrong. It was more than just a puzzle. It was someone's death.

By the time he had locked up his bicycle and

pulled open the heavy glass entrance doors of the Municipal Building, his involvement in the case had shifted on to a different plane. Last night he had gone home to a leisurely late dinner, and afterwards had read for half an hour a novel he had started two days earlier. But now he concluded that he shouldn't have done that, that while this murderer was free he was not justified in indulging in the pleasures of a normal life. Hilda Robertson's normal life had been interrupted, and as a matter of right his should be interrupted, too. He was, after all, the relevant law enforcement officer.

It was just before eight and Mary Underwood hadn't come in yet, at least she wasn't in the office, but Constanza saw that Sam Dawson's door was closed. He knocked and entered and found Lionel Friedman, in blue jeans and rumpled button-down shirt, staring up at him.

Sam Dawson was lounging back in his chair behind the desk and spoke to Constanza. 'Mr Friedman here calls me up ten minutes ago very anxious about seeing you, so I invited him over. I told him you wouldn't mind. He says he knew Hilda Robertson very slightly, thinks he bought her coffee once—'

Friedman held up a cautionary finger. 'Or a Coke. It may have been a Coke.'

Dawson nodded. 'Or a Coke. He also thinks that his lost library card may be somehow connected to this murder, maybe connecting *him* to this murder—'

Friedman held up his finger again. 'In a way that I really don't know.'

'And,' continued Dawson, 'he wants to know if he's in trouble. Says he was up half the night wondering if he was in trouble.'

'What did you tell him?' said Constanza expressionlessly.

Dawson's eyes flicked at Constanza and must have found something there because he frowned for a second. Then: 'I told him he could be. He's just told me that he was sleeping in his room at the time of the murder. Alone.'

'That means no alibi,' said Constanza.

Dawson turned to Friedman. 'You see, Mr Friedman? Now you tell *me* if you might be in trouble. Better yet, why don't you tell us again how you came to lose your library card?'

'Well, really, all I know is that I must have lost it on May the tenth. Except I can't tell you how. Or where. I really can't. I know it had to be the tenth because I applied for a new one on the eleventh, and you really can't do anything here at the University without the library. And I know I was spending some time at the library practically every day at around that time. So it had to be around the tenth. Listen, is the exact date all that crucial?'

'Do you have a lawyer, Mr Friedman?' said Dawson.

'Oh, Christ, no,' said Friedman. 'Are you telling me that I should get one?' He ran his left hand nervously through his hair, and then shook his head once. 'You know, I don't even think my folks have one,' he said softly. Suddenly he looked up. His face had paled. 'Listen, I'm on fifty per cent financial aid here. Is that going to be affected by any of this?'

'That's purely a University matter, Mr Friedman,' said Dawson. 'So far there is no official connection between you and this investigation apart from the fact that we have spoken to you. We don't notify the registrar's office or the Dean of Students or anything like that. Of course, that could change. If, for example, we were forced to issue a warrant for your arrest, even if only for questioning as a material or an uncooperative witness, we would have to notify the University. I have no idea what their rules are here, but it's something you might want to keep in mind. So if there's anything more you want to tell us, now would be the time. Withholding relevant information is generally considered to be obstructing justice. Otherwise we have no more questions just now, and you can go.'

Lionel Friedman was clearly put out. He licked his lips, swallowed, and remained seated with his head lowered in thought. Dawson waited patiently for a few moments, then leaned forward. 'Mr Friedman? Anything you want to say?'

Friedman's head jerked up, a fierce frown on his face. 'I'm thinking, OK? Just give me a second,' he said testily. He lowered his head again; then, after a couple of moments, shook it morosely. 'No.

No, I really can't. If there were I'd sure as hell tell
you, but there isn't. Christ.'

'That'll be fine, Mr Friedman. Just keep us in
mind. As we will be keeping you in mind. You got
any questions, Phil?'

Constanza returned Friedman's gaze seriously.
'No, not right now. But I think he should keep
himself available. Not make any long trips without
notifying us, right?'

'Right,' said Friedman. 'I understand. Look, if I
do I'll call you. You can depend on that, OK?' He
got up to leave. 'Is there anything else I should
do?'

'No,' said Dawson. 'That's all for now.'

Friedman turned and left.

Dawson waited until he had closed the door,
then immediately turned to Constanza and said,
'Everything OK with you Phil? Nothing the matter,
is there?'

'No,' said Constanza. 'Well, maybe yes. I'm not
sure. I was riding in this morning on the bike, and
I got to thinking and I guess I just got a little mad.
At me, at the killer. It was a very strong personal
reaction, Sam. He killed somebody, right? Well,
we should be more serious about this. You know
what I mean?'

Dawson didn't know exactly what to say. 'What
are you suggesting, Phil?'

'Oh, I don't know. Maybe we shouldn't be so
casual about everything.'

Dawson's eyes narrowed slightly. 'I'm not casual, Phil. I don't think you are, either. You think we're selling anybody short here? I don't. You begin to be too self-conscious about what you're doing, begin to take yourself too seriously, you can get into trouble. You want to talk about this?'

Constanza looked at the air over Dawson's head, then compressed his lips and shook his head. 'No, Sam, I don't. Look, I don't even know exactly what the hell I mean.' He stopped, then took a deep breath. 'Can we please just forget about all this? I'm beginning to sound like an idiot to myself.'

Dawson made a point of shrugging his shoulders. 'Sure. Listen, you got anything on for the rest of this morning?'

'Well, I want to use the phone a little, talk to some people, line up some people. Robertson's parents, some of her friends, Beecham's wife, McCardle. He usually knows a hell of a lot of what goes on in this town.'

'McCardle's a good idea,' said Sam. 'I hadn't thought of that. And don't forget, we should leave here by eleven. Maybe have some lunch before we hit the Trenton Police Lab.'

Constanza finished his telephoning almost exactly at eleven and waited until they were in Dawson's car heading for Trenton before telling him that Beecham's wife had said that she had been up reading until eleven-thirty Monday night and, as far as she knew, Professor Beecham did *not* spend the night there.

# THIRTEEN

'TENURE IS A MARVELLOUS invention, a perfect example of privilege inventing its own rules. It provides for security in general and self-perpetuation in particular. It is the single most effective carrot-and-stick I know. It's effective because it is simultaneously carrot *and* stick, and because it is really the only condition sufficient for an academic career; not competence, not age, not experience, only tenure. Presidents can be impeached, governors and mayors can be recalled, CEOs can be stock-voted out, kings can be beheaded, dictators can be overthrown. All these are child's play compared to getting rid of a tenured professor. The reason is perfectly simple; we're all afraid of precedent or that some day we ourselves may be threatened. It's a common thread, a unifying outlook. We are the strongest union in the world. We are one terrific closed society and we let in only those we want to. And we are very, very careful about it.'

'Tell me, Professor Smith-Kohlmer,' said Dawson, 'can the Department head make tenured appointments?'

They were standing on the patio just to the left

of the French doors through which they had just strolled. Professor Wilfred Smith-Kohlmer held a plastic plate of bitesized pieces of beef teriyaki on a bed of soft rice noodles. A stamped-out well in the plate securely held a plastic glass of Beaujolais. He was eating rapidly even as he spoke. Dawson held a similar plate but loaded with sweet and sour shrimp with white rice and beer. They had sidled off to the left so as not to interfere with the traffic that was now moving from the large sitting-room of Professor Beecham's house outside into a pleasantly warm late afternoon sun. There was a good half-acre of well-tended lawn here spotted with the occasional white garden table and chairs. The two full and four associate professors who formed the nucleus of the Art Department at Kingsford University had concluded the business part of the their meeting which had started at two-thirty and covered the evaluation of the year just finishing and plans for the year ahead.

Dawson and Constanza had duly arrived at four-thirty as bidden, and were asked by Professor Beecham to wait, please, for five minutes. The trip to the Trenton Police Labs had been a total zero (except that Constanza had done some good networking and made a couple of good contacts), and the drive back to Kingsford had for the most part been silent. Constanza had forgotten all about the buckwheat pancake flour. Waiting for Beecham, even for five minutes, didn't help their humour any.

'Well, not exactly,' Smith-Kohlmer was saying.

'Tenure is granted to an individual, never less than an Associate Professor, after a departmental committee recommends it to a university-wide tenure committee which then recommends to the Dean of Faculty. The department head chairs the departmental committee and usually makes the initial recommendation. Generally speaking, any objection along the line, any official objection, is enough to block the appointment.'

'Tell me, are there occasionally any, ah, heated discussions during the process?' asked Dawson as he popped a shrimp into his mouth.

Smith-Kohlmer threw his head back and laughed. 'Mr Dawson, there are always heated discussions. Often there are vicious words, sometimes there is a surprisingly intense animosity, occasionally there are threats, and twice to my knowledge physical restraint had to be used. Oh my, the stories. But you see, these meetings never see the light of day. Indeed, there are never any minutes taken of such meetings; the names of the approved nominees are the only things made public. You couldn't have it any other way, could you now?'

'I guess not. But seriously, Professor, is there anything you could tell me that might, just might, prove helpful in assisting our search for who the murderer of that poor girl might be?' Dawson had continued jockeying away from the main group of people and they were standing well off to a side by now. 'I know that this is not pleasant for anyone but, for example, was there jealousy over Miss

Robertson's appointment? Was there, uh, reaction to the, uh, circumstances of the appointment?'

Smith-Kohlmer's face became solemn. He looked away for a moment, not eating, his eyes focused on the middle distance. Then he turned and looked back directly at Dawson. 'She was a nice girl, you know. Pleasant. A hard worker. A willing worker. Competent enough. No, not outstanding, not brilliant, but above average.' He paused, then, shaking his head slightly, continued. 'You know, Mr Dawson, nothing like this has ever happened so close to me. We had actually eaten lunch together several times. I mean, we were in the same Department.' He looked down at his plate and seemed not to see his food there. He looked up. 'Yes, there was jealousy. Jealousy and resentment. Of both the appointment and the circumstances.' He leaned towards Dawson a bit. His mouth became stern and he spoke in a lowered, yet firmer voice. 'The appointment was clearly out of line. Much too young, no degree, no publishing record. And there was no secret about her liaison with Beecham. I mean, that sort of thing does go on. And, to be honest about it, it's generally tolerated. A peccadillo. One shrugs one's shoulders and smiles indulgently and hopes that no hurt results. There's usually very little to go on for apportioning blame accurately in these matters. But, yes, an appointment like this in the given circumstances rankles.' He paused and absent-mindedly took a sip of wine. 'But, good Lord, killing.' He shook his head. 'Good Lord.'

'Look, Professor, I know that this may not be exactly the right occasion but I'd like to give you my number and ask you to please think about things and give me a call at any time if anything occurs to you. Often in cases like this, time can be of the essence. And you never can tell what may turn out to be important. Is that all right with you?'

'Yes, of course that will be all right with me. Anything really to get to the bottom of this terrible situation.'

He took the card Dawson had proffered him and put it in his vest pocket. Dawson thanked him and began to circulate about the lawn, searching for one of the younger-looking faculty members there to see what story *he* would tell him. He passed close to Constanza in conversation with a furiously gesticulating man and made a point not to stop.

Constanza, in fact, had to keep backing away from Professor Stefan Lupescu to avoid being brushed by the tip of an imported cigarillo that was firmly implanted into the end of a six-inch gold-and-ivory cigarette holder. Lupescu wore a very lightweight, almost translucent straw hat with a turned-down brim, a beige Italian silk jacket worn over the shoulders like a cape, and a dark blue silk foulard knotted and tucked into an open-necked light blue shirt. His face consisted mostly of a pair of bushy, grey eyebrows and a similarly bushy grey moustache positioned respectively above and below a red-veined slightly bulbous nose. His voice covered the range from contra-tenor to baritone and covered it often. There was more than a hint of eau-de-cologne about him.

'It is incredible to me, totally incredible, that Hollywood has not yet made a movie of Michelangelo Merisi da Caravaggio. Robert de Niro, with his dark good looks, was born, *born,* to play him. My God, what a man he was! And what a life! Listen, my friend, how about this. Just listen. Arrives in Rome out of nowhere—actually from the town of Caravaggio near Brescia—gets apprenticed to one of the academic schools of painting and immediately becomes the crudely talented, arrogant rebel. Paints in rooms where he illuminates people by hanging a lantern off to a side because that's how they actually lived then, and that's what their lives would actually look like. Coarse, powerful pictures of stark contrasts, half of a face sharply lit, the other half in strongly shadowed background. Then the usual patronage of a rich and powerful cleric. Next, commissions and the usual rumours of homosexuality. Well, actually *facts* of homosexuality. Then begins to paint the reality of the people and the streets of the times. Cheating card-players, leering whisperers, shoppers with torn sleeves. Eventually, of course, turns to religious themes and immediately, but immediately, attracts the total wrath of the clergy. You know why? You know what their complaint was?' He leaned forward, waving his cigarillo, forcing Constanza back two more steps. 'Their complaint was that he painted his religious figures and subjects on the levels of everyday life. Painted faces of Mary and Peter that could be seen in the alleys of Naples and Rome. None of this ethereal, vacant-eyed, other-worldly shit for him. No, the clergy complained that his religious faces were too human, too *human*, no less. And all this—*all* this at the end of the sixteenth century. Can you imagine?

'And his life! Listen to this, my friend. Joins a pick-up tennis match in Rome, gets into a brawl with one of the players and kills him. Has to flee. Spends the rest of his life wandering around the Mediterranean. Malta, Sicily, Naples. Literally paints on the run. Gets into trouble with a Maltese Knight who promptly swears a vendetta and pursues him all the way back to Italy. Caravaggio, just one step ahead of him most of the time, finally eludes him only to be ultimately arrested in a case of mistaken identity. Escapes again, but now penniless, roams the beaches, contracts a fever and dies. Do you conceive, Sergeant, of the movie? The combination of the religious, the artistic, the mundane, and the symbolic. Let alone the actual. And, of course, the clashes among all these. Why has no one out there thought of this? Small minds, Sergeant, totally small minds. They put Charlton Heston in a Michelangelo movie. Hah! Small minds.' He removed the cigarillo stub from his holder, flicked it away and put the holder into an inside breast pocket. Suddenly he drew himself up and gathered his jacket more closely about his shoulders. 'As to being of any help with your investigation, I'm afraid I can be of no use to you. I know nothing.' He turned on his heel and abruptly strode off, leaving Constanza gaping after him.

'Don't let him throw you,' said a voice off to a side, 'he's just being Lupescu.' The voice came from a man at a nearby garden table that had an umbrella mounted on a pole through its centre. The speaker was a round-faced, pug-nosed, well-freckled man in his mid-thirties with the remains of a meal on the paper plate before him. He was sipping a glass of white wine and smiling.

Constanza strolled over and sat down. 'Is he that way with everyone?'

'Everyone except Beecham. He's a perfect example of an old-world, central European's overbearing arrogance to subordinates and underbearing obsequiousness to superiors.' He offered a hand which Constanza took and said, 'I'm Flynn, associate prof, relatively new. Been here three years. I can talk this way because I know that nobody in the department likes him and I recently got tenured. Doubly protected, you might say. And since you're investigating the murder, I think it's something you should know.'

'Did Miss Robertson dislike him, too?'

'Yes, but you've got to remember that to Lupescu she was too—' he searched for a word— 'inconsequential for him to notice.'

'Well then, uh, how does a guy like Lupescu operate in an atmosphere like this?'

'By being the brightest luminary in the Department. Look, I came here from McGill up in Montreal because, believe it or not, Lupescu was here. Let me tell you something, Constanza. If you asked any art historian from Berkely to Leningrad to list the five best art historians in the field, the one single name guaranteed to be on everyone's list would be Lupescu's. He's the Enrico Fermi of Art History. He's both theoretical and practical. He knows where things are, how to access them, what socio-political-cultural tracts bear on them, what other historians have said about them. He is, in the most literal sense, a walking encyclopaedia. He churns out consistently high quality papers at an astonishing rate. He has helped me enormously. He has helped others enormously. The Department wanted him so badly that they prevailed upon the library to hire his wife as the assistant curator of its Eastern European special collection. It's common knowledge that he's made this Department the front-runner for the first Horace E. Fernwood endowed chair in Art History. We're talking genuine international plum here, in addition to a $250,000 annual grant. So that's who Stefan Lupescu is.'

Constanza sipped his by now warm vodka-tonic. 'Tell me, Professor, is he gay?'

'Yes, he is,' came the prompt, matter-of-fact reply, 'but neither he nor anyone else makes a major point of it. His wife, by the way, is a second cousin of his. Interesting story there. It seems that both their families were smuggled out of Romania when they were teenagers. Lupescu made it to London where, in fact, he began his career. But the other family ran out of money and got hung up in Budapest. One day, out of the blue, two years after the Hungarian uprising, he's given her address by one of the thousands of refugees this country let in from there. Seems she belonged to a clandestine political group; and, you must remember, while politics here is TV spots and voting booths, over there it's blood in the streets. So on his next trip to central Europe he looks her up in Budapest. Turns out she's his last surviving relative. Chief librarian at the State University. Well, apparently the celebrated strong ties of the East European family are all too true because one day, out for a carefully planned idle stroll past the American Embassy, he whisks her inside where she asks for, and gets, political asylum. He marries her on the spot. An American passport is waiting for her, complete with entry visa corresponding to Lupescu's and in three hours they are on a TWA flight on their way to Rome. Nobody at the airport sees fit to question them because there was no reason to. Just like a movie. Once here, her marriage licence gives her instant legal status and everybody chooses not to make a fuss. End of story. By the way, I hear that the Eastern Europe collection is very happy with her. I've met her a few times and found her to be a charming and highly cultured lady. She sort of acts the official hostess for Lupescu's social functions. And, yes, she also acts as his cover.'

Constanza must have looked entranced because Flynn smiled suddenly and said, 'And you know, Sergeant, the single most interesting thing about this story is that only the Americans seem surprised by it.'

Constanza nodded, then asked, 'Is there anything at all you can tell me about the killing?'

'I wish I could, Sergeant. You know by now about her shacking up with Beecham and her—ah—unusually early promotion, right?'

'Right.'

'Then you know as much as I do. More, I'm sure. I really hardly knew the girl.'

Constanza noticed Dawson trying to catch his eye. 'Last question. Do you know anyone in the Department, or outside, who might have any information for me?'

'Not that I can think of. Look, give me a number where I can reach you and if I do think of anything I'll give you a call, OK?'

'Thanks, Professor. We need all the help we can get on this.'

Constanza rose and gave him a card. Across the lawn he saw Dawson doing the same thing to a small group he had been conversing with. Now he looked at Constanza, pointed to his wristwatch and jerked his head towards the door. It was after five and they hadn't yet gone over what to say at today's press conference; Constanza guessed they would be doing that on their drive back to the Kingsford Inn.

On their way to the car Constanza asked Dawson if he had learned anything. 'Only that people with tenure can be ruled out as suspects because of lack of professional motive,' he said. 'Of course, that says nothing about personal or romantic motive.'

'And that,' said Constanza, 'probably goes double for Lupescu.'

They got into the car and started back. Constanza drove while Dawson talked.

'Listen, Phil,' said Dawson, 'the reporters have now had one full day of nosing around on their own, and the combination of their own skills and the fact that people like to be paid attention to has almost certainly given them Robertson's affair with Beecham. I suggest we give them that tonight and also her unusually early promotion.' Constanza started to object but Dawson cut him off. 'Listen, these guys are no slouches. It's all out there in public and at least one of them is going to look at possible favouritism here and come up with that. So let's give it to them. And there's another reason. We don't want to run the risk of looking like complete idiots, and the fact is we should have come up with anything like that ourselves by now. So let's tell 'em. Because I don't want to tell them about Friedman or the lost library card or the book checkouts or about her other boyfriend. At least, not yet, anyhow. So we tell 'em about our unpro-

ductive trip to the Trenton Labs, the lack of any
forensic findings anyplace and no clear definite
suspects yet. And finally that we're following up
on some promising leads that we feel we really
can't divulge at this time. All this OK with you?'

Constanza nodded.

'No reservations?'

'No, really. I think you're right on all these matters.'

'Good. Because that's how I wrote up the hand-
outs for this evening. Oh, and before I forget. Go
over the articles in today's newspapers. I know you
didn't get a chance today, but be sure you do before you turn in tonight. There's no telling what
you might pick up or what ideas you can get from
someone else's write-up of what you've done. A
question of perspective. The *Chronicle*'s the most
complete. Incidentally, only the *Chronicle* and the
*Trenton Times* put it on page one. The other majors
had it inside on pages two, three or four, although
the *New York Times* had it on the first page of its
New Jersey section.' Dawson suddenly looked at
Constanza. 'You getting all this, Phil? I mean,
we've got less than ten minutes and I've got to
stop by the office for messages.'

'Not to worry, Sam. I've got it all and I agree
with it all.'

There was only one message of real interest that
Dawson got from Mary Underwood. It was long
but it made Dawson smile broadly.

'It seems,' said Dawson, 'that the *Post* guy

tracked down that Twelvetrees girl and began to follow her around and take pictures of her. I mean, hell, she *is* a looker. So finally, she got into a car with him and told him to leave her alone or she would rip her blouse and report him for attempted rape and assault. He quit immediately and she left the message to let us know that that's the real story just in case any of it comes out. Smart girl. I like that. Christ, I sure hope she's not implicated in this. I might want to take her out after all this is over.'

They pulled into the Kingsford Inn's parking lot. 'Well, right on time. Just you and me, Phil. Ready?'

'Ready, Sam.'

It lasted only twenty minutes, and there was a clear feeling of restlessness in the room. Reporters from the Baltimore and Washington papers didn't even show. Dawson actually apologized at the end for the lack of progress but said that much of the legwork which, he reminded the reporters, forms the backbone of any such investigation, had yet to be done. Constanza's supper was earlier than he had expected and actually overlapped the kids' meal a little. But he made up for the unanticipated pleasure by assiduously going over with a coloured highlighting pencil the collection of Wednesday's newspapers Dawson had given him in his office. It took him until eleven-thirty.

Finally, just before turning in, Constanza listed the appointments he had planned for the following day—McCardle, Beecham's wife, Hilda Robertson's parents, her as yet unknown boyfriend—and their approximate time slots.

He could have saved himself the trouble.

# FOURTEEN

PROFESSOR Alardyce Stallings had spent thousands of hours in libraries. Their tall, booklined walls and long rows of publications on open racks had always exuded a hospitality that seemed to hug him and hold him snug, even in the coldest of British winters. The volumes themselves were, to him, individual packets of soft delight, immediately responsive to his opening touch and subsequently devoured through greedy eyes and grasping brain. Foreign lands, alien faces, other lives, all surrounded him in libraries. Ships, tastes, cities, thoughts, the sheer naked power of information, were all available to him in libraries. Over the years of his life since the age of seven, when his family had moved from a Cornish fishing village to Bristol, the library had evolved from a place of wondrous discovery to the place of his life's work. As far back as he could remember, library work had been accompanied by a never-wavering, pervasive pleasure. To this day, his heart rose when he entered a library and, often without realizing it, his face smiled. In the matter of libraries, he and Philip Constanza were boughs from the same tree.

The early folios were all kept in one section, the

northwest corner of A-level, one storey below ground. As usual, Stallings took the elevator down. He had been riding down and walking up ever since his knee cartilage gave out about fifteen years ago. His knees had given him more than half a century of tennis, skiing and gardening and Stallings had no real cause for complaint. His knees had, he felt, given him a fine enough run. But, Lord, they were stiff in the mornings now.

He put his notebook and two pens on his usual work table and went to get the two earliest of the three folios of *Richard the Third* that the library had acquired over the last hundred years. He was well into his latest project now, relating the differences in these three manuscripts to the political history of the early seventeenth century. He had found an absolutely delicious packet of letters between two attendees of a meeting of royal historians at Tunbridge Wells in 1638 discussing the ramifications of writing official history during the shift from a Tudor to a Stuart Court. It was precisely the sort of thing that Stallings did best. It was all speculation, of course, nothing concrete, and he would be the first to admit that his interpretations were occasionally quite personal. But his justifications were always well-argued and generally well-received. It was his *métier,* he did it well and he delighted in it.

It was only eight-thirty and he looked forward to at least a three-, possibly a four-hour session. He removed his candy bar from his shirt pocket and placed it at the side of the table. If habit were to be followed it would be eaten in about two hours. Stallings had grown accustomed to his candy bars during his early school years, as had much of Britain's younger citizenry, and by the time he had reached the age of fifty most of his teeth were no longer his own. He remembered reading once that England's sweet tooth was costing the National Health over two billion pounds a year and supporting many a dentist.

He carefully opened the folios and the packet of letters and experienced again the familiar anticipation brought on by the mustiness and brittleness of the pages before him. It was almost sensual, like the first deep aroma of a woman's body coming up from under the just-loosened sweater, or the first vibrant odours of a fresh tomato-and-basil sauce as the waiter sets down the steaming platter of pasta. Well, he philosophized contentedly, he had had a fine enough run at some of those things, too.

He worked steadily for about two hours and was just leaning forward to get his sweet when he heard a faint swishing noise behind him and suddenly everything around him—Shakespeare folios, seventeenth-century correspondence, sweet—was transformed into a searing, world-filling pain at the back of his head. It seemed to him, oddly, that he actually heard the blow *after* the pain, a distinct thunk, and his last clear thought was to wonder how that was possible. He fell sideways to the floor, and the numbness where the blow had struck began rapidly to spread through his head. But he did not lose consciousness immediately and so was able to feel recurrent blows to his body. These were not sharp, as the first blow to the head had been, but were massive and dull. He tried to raise his right arm protectively, but simply couldn't. Then the spreading numbness reached his eyes and closed down the light, and the next things he was conscious of were the sounds of soft moaning, a continuing inability to move, and feeling very cold. He knew he lay like that for some time before he felt hands moving over his body and began to hear vague shouting sounds off in a distance.

'HELLO, PHIL? Sam. Get yourself awake enough to listen. Take your time. I'll wait a little.'

'Uh, yeah, yeah, OK.' Constanza forced three deep breaths into his lungs. 'Look, let me pick up in the kitchen. Sally's still asleep here. Hold on a few seconds, OK?'

'Sure, Phil. Good idea.'

Constanza slipped on a pair of boxer shorts and a T-shirt and padded down the hall past the bathroom (that would have to wait now) and into the kitchen where he picked up the wall phone.

'OK, Sam, what's up?' He scratched his face and noted the luminous red numbers on the microwave clock. Christ, four-thirty.

'Listen, Phil, sorry to bother you and all but

there's been an assault over at the University. In the library.'

'In the library?' said Constanza.

'Yeah, in the library. An old retired guy. Professor Alardyce Stallings. Seventy-seven years old. Used to be in English Lit. Beaten very badly with, like, a bat or a lead pipe. Found about an hour ago, moaning, in a small pool of blood by a roving security guard making rounds. He was in a corner, out of the usual traffic lanes. The blood was already beginning to congeal when he was found. Looks to have happened a few hours ago. He's not dead but pretty damned close.' Dawson paused. 'You OK, Phil? You getting this?'

'Yeah, I'm fine. Really. Go on, Sam.'

'Well, listen. He's at the hospital now. They've fixed him up and he's conscious, but just. The doc over there, the resident on duty, guy named Starbuck, says he probably won't last long. The only thing Stallings has said so far was that he didn't see who did it. I was going to go over there and question him myself but I've changed my mind. Instead, I'm going to call up everybody connected with the Robertson killing right now and find out where they were around midnight. I'm also going to take over some of the legwork you had scheduled for today. I want you to go over to the hospital to question Stallings and see what you can get. This way you'll at least get your information first hand and see if you can find any connections with the Robertson thing. And, anyhow, you've been doing most of the questioning on this case yourself. What d'you say?'

'Right.' Constanza was fully awake now. 'So you think it's all connected, right?'

'Who knows for sure, but yeah, I think it's all connected. Shit, it damn well better be. The alternative would mean two separate and independent murders in the Kingsford University library in the space of two days. Chew that over on your way to the hospital.'

'Yeah, I see what you mean. OK, I'm on my way. What was the doc's name again?'

'Starbuck. He'll probably be hanging around the emergency room this time of day. Night. Whatever. I'll call and tell him you're coming.'

Constanza hung up, went to the bathroom and while urinating tried to remember if he had heard of a Professor Stallings. The name was familiar but he couldn't put his finger on anything. He quickly pulled on a pair of jeans and an old rugby shirt, scribbled a note for Sally and hurried to his car.

Half way to the hospital it came to him. A front-page article in the *Chronicle*. Professor Alardyce Stallings had received an award from the National Shakespeare Society for his work on the early Shakespeare folios two years ago and had been designated Professor Emeritus at the University. The point had been made that he was still actively continuing his studies.

He drove directly to the emergency room entrance located by a cluster of lighted windows and doors surrounded by the dark mass of the rest of the Kingsford Hospital. Dr Starbuck was waiting for him, leaning against the door jamb of the ambulance entrance. He was slim, half a head taller than Constanza, with a swarthy skin sufficiently at odds with sandy hair and light blue eyes that you couldn't help but notice. They introduced themselves and Starbuck led him quickly through an emergency room in which tables, countertops, wall cabinets, sinks, utensils—everything—seemed to be made of stainless steel. They passed through another room, adjunct to the emergency room and smaller, containing a row of curtained cots on large roller wheels, and then, finally, to a small office with 'Duty Resident' painted on its door. Starbuck picked up some papers from a cluttered desk but he had actually begun talking back in the emergency room.

'Now the first thing you've got to know is that Stallings is in a very bad way. From his blood pressure and pulse he's lost an awful lot of blood, not so much externally—there wasn't much seen, I was told—as internally. He almost certainly has a ruptured spleen, and other internal injuries as well. Lots of palpable abdominal swelling. He's at least a little shocky. He's getting plasma but it's not helping. He's received blows to the head as well as the body and likely has a skull fracture, although no X-rays have been taken. The man who did this was clearly trying to kill him and just as clearly made a mess of it. Stallings is seventy-seven, frail, and in his present state wouldn't stand a chance of surviving the surgery required to repair his internal injuries even if they were repairable and even if I could get a team together in half an hour.' He halted momentarily and sighed deeply. If he were smoking, thought Constanza, this would be the time for a slow, thoughtful drag.

But he wasn't smoking. Starbuck looked directly into Constanza's eyes. 'There's really,' he said, 'absolutely nothing to be done. He's floating in and out of consciousness with a continuing decline over the past thirty minutes. I've made him as comfortable as I can and—' He stopped suddenly and leaned forward. His voice took on an edge. 'Listen, Constanza, I could put him in an Intensive Care cubicle, attach wires and gauges to him, and thoroughly monitor his dying, right? Instead, I've doped him up so that he feels no pain, put him in a bright private room where he can see into the park if he lasts till dawn, and I've dug up some nice-looking flowers to scatter around the room. I'm telling you all this because I presume you'll be wanting to ask him some questions, and I want you to know what's going on, OK?'

'That's fine, Dr Starbuck,' said Constanza. 'I understand exactly what you're telling me and I appreciate it. Will you show me to his room now? If it weren't really important, I wouldn't be doing this now. You understand that, I hope.'

'Right,' said Starbuck. 'Let's go.'

They took an elevator to the third floor, walked

past a nurse's station and turned a corner. 'Number three-nineteen, on the right. I'll be either at the nurse's station here or in the emergency room, OK?'

'Fine,' said Constanza. 'I'll be sure to check with you before I leave. And thanks again.'

Starbuck hesitated, then said, 'This has to do with that girl's murder, right, Sergeant?'

'Right,' said Constanza. 'At least, we think it does.'

Starbuck nodded, turned, and left.

Constanza had been in hospital corridors many times, of course, but he had never gotten used to it and probably never would. It had always seemed to him to be well outside the normally defined planes of life, a sort of limbo place between life and—what? Constanza started down the corridor.

At night, deserted as they usually are, it's positively eerie. You become aware of things that you're not ordinarily aware of. Sounds are louder, for example, and they belong to things generally not thought of, like the vibrational humming of electrical equipment or the soft sibilance of some pneumatic machinery. As you walk past open doors, you can hear much more closely the almost continuous nocturnal stirrings and shiftings of bodies, and a sudden cough three rooms away is like a rifle shot. Everything seems amplified by the unnatural absence of voices and footsteps.

You pass these rooms knowing that the people in them are different. Planned and purposeful violence has been done to them, cuttings, sawings, stitchings, needle punctures, fluids forced in and out of the openings. Germs and viruses are at work, and white blood cells, too, all operating at activity levels far above the normal. For the lucky ones, it's a temporary state fashioned to improve their bodies. But there are unlucky ones, too.

Professor Stallings lay propped up on two pillows in the only lighted room along the corridor. Flowers were everywhere, on the bureau and on chairs placed close to the bed and under the windows. Reds and yellows and whites. An enormous bouquet of roses in a background of rich green ferns was on a food cart positioned over Stallings's legs so that he couldn't help seeing them. Stallings's eyes were, in fact, open but not focused. An IV tube was taped to a scrawny forearm. A bandage slanted loosely across his forehead. More bandages, visible through a thin hospital gown, bulked around his chest. His breathing was shallow and occasionally softly vocal. The smell of disinfectant was strong in the air.

The skin behind Constanza's scrotum crawled.

He leaned forward and called out softly, 'Professor Stallings? Professor Stallings. Please, can you hear me? Sir?'

Constanza removed some flowers from a chair and sat down close to Stallings's side. Slowly, Stallings blinked once, then moved only his eyes to him, and then, again slowly, turned his head towards him. After several seconds he said, 'Yes, young man, I can hear you.'

Constanza felt bad about not wanting to waste time, but didn't let it stop him. 'Professor Stallings, I'm from the police investigating this case. Tell me, sir, did you see who did this to you?'

'No, young man, I did not.'

'Did you see anything about the man, a sweater, a tie, a ring, shoes, anything at all?'

Stallings paused, but his eyes remained focused. 'That was good, young man. I don't think the other men, either the man that found me or the doctor, asked me that. Shoes were brown moccasin type. Not shirt cuffs visible, and no tie. Could be a sweater or a turtleneck. Some dark colour. No smell, no sound, no face. Just surprise and pain. No pain now, thank you. Some vibration in my head, though, and a little nausea.' He took a breath.

At first, Stallings's voice had been quavering and unsteady, but as he spoke it strengthened. Even so, he talked in a monotone and with a minimum of muscle movement about the face, as though to husband his energy. 'Doing some work on our first folio of Richard Three. Just reaching for my sweet when he struck me. No sound, no sound at all. Deserted, couldn't—'

'Professor Stallings, what time was it, sir?'

There was silence for a while. Stallings's eyes, like blue marbles, began to drift away, to move in slightly different directions. Then they focused again and returned to Constanza. 'Don't know really. Late, though.'

'Sir, please, how late?'

'I would guess elevenish-twelvish.'

Constanza was making jottings in a small pocket-sized notebook.

'Sir, can you think of any reason, any reason at all, why anyone would want to…to…do this to you?'

Stallings's lips worked and took on an asymmetric broadening that Constanza could easily extrapolate to an attractive smile. Even in his current condition there were strong traces of irony in his voice. 'Am I dying, young man?'

Constanza was stunned. Christ, what could he say. He did know that the one thing he could not do was pause. He forced words into his mouth. 'I don't think so, Professor. You've been badly hurt, but no, I don't think so. Uh, about the reason for this—'

'No, young man, not a trace, not a clue. Haven't the foggiest.' The voice was still soft, but firmer now, and with good articulation. Could Starbuck have been wrong?

It seemed to Constanza that there wasn't very much more he could hope to get from Stallings, so he went without further delay to the only really pertinent question all this could possibly be leading to. 'Professor Stallings, can you think of any connection between this attack and the death of that girl in the library two days ago?'

This time the smile was unequivocal, and Constanza could sense, almost see in his mind, a sparkling eye. 'You're giving yourself away, young man. Most unseemly haste. Beginning to sound as though you're in a clear hurry, as though you're questioning a dying man. Well, no need to fret.' His eyes, half open but none the less lively, now suddenly closed. But his breathing remained regular, although shallow. Constanza waited. How could he be so lucid, talk so well, have such a clear mind in his state? Well, he had lived a life of the mind, hadn't he? Built a life of scholarship in the almost one thousand years of English Literature with a long stopover at the early folios of Shakespeare. And he was still active at seventy-seven— right up to about six hours ago.

Constanza didn't know if Stallings were sleeping or resting or whatever. A blue vein in his temple pulsed regularly. That and the slow rise and fall of his stomach were the only indications of life. Constanza studied the man. Definitely slim, but with his regular features, still nicely trimmed moustache, good head of hair, and of course that hint of a smile that looked as though it would have devastated the girls, Professor Alardyce Stallings looked every inch the attractive British don in his winter years. Well, all coming to a close, now.

Constanza shook his head. Bastard. Goddamned bastard. Stabbing and clubbing. Where do such people learn that? First, to stick a knife into someone's throat, and then to smash a head.

It was fully ten minutes before Stallings opened his eyes, but when he did it was to continue the conversation as though without interruption. 'Well, it is connected, of course, but I really don't know how. My feeling is that the man thought I did know something and acted quite desperately. Except—' he smiled weakly again—'I don't know what the blazes it is. Genuinely sorry, young man. Truly.'

Stallings shifted his hands from across his stomach to his sides. Constanza leaned forward. 'Is there anything I can do, Professor? Anything I can get for you?'

'Perhaps a sip of water, please.'

Constanza paused an instant. Internal injuries, Starbuck had said. Was Stallings not supposed to get water? Sometimes water was prohibited. Starbuck hadn't said anything about that. But hell, the man was doped up, dying, thirsty. He looked around, found a tray on the bureau with a pitcher, glasses and straws and poured Stallings a drink, holding the straw for him. Stallings nodded his thanks. Again he closed his eyes, but this time only for a few seconds. When he opened them, he looked first directly at Constanza, then slowly around the room at the flowers. He sighed. Whether it was resignation or to gather strength, Constanza couldn't say.

Stallings's eyes returned to Constanza's face. 'I must say the girls were something. Not lately, of course, but when I was younger. Had my share, I suppose. Perhaps more than my share.' He smiled softly. 'Lovely, lovely things, their naked bodies. Truly beautiful. Even the not-so-beautiful girls became somehow beautiful when naked. Ever notice that, young man? Loved them all, really I did.' He rested a moment. 'Didn't like the homosexuals.' He pronounced it *hahmaseckshuls.* 'Knew a lot of them, y'know. Here at the University, other universities, both in and out of closets. Had my chances, I s'pose. Thought about it a bit, but in the end always no. Never. Never could tell where they were coming from. All the same, terribly creative, truly gifted.'

He stopped again, and his shoulders slumped a little on the pillow, as though from exertion. His eyes lost focus once more, and Constanza, in what he would later say was the single most spontaneous gesture of his life, suddenly reached out and took Stallings's hand firmly in his. For a moment he felt an answering pressure. Then the translucent fingers relaxed. Constanza leaned forward, apprehensive. But he could still see that pulse going in the temple. Stallings's breathing seemed to become shallower, though still steady. Constanza wanted to release Stallings's hand, but feared disturbing him if he were sleeping or resting. Resting for what, he thought, for dying?

But again, after a moment or two, Stallings opened his eyes and moved his fingers within Constanza's. For a couple of seconds he stared, glassy-eyed, at the opposite wall, then slowly focused on Constanza's face. Suddenly, two spots of colour incongruously appeared high up on his cheek-bones, and his eyes moved to the window, clearly grey now with the light of the coming dawn. His eyes and the pulse in his temple were the only things that moved now.

'Please put out the room lights, young man.'

Constanza rose, switched off the lights and returned to again take up Stallings's hand. He felt again the answering, thankful pressure.

'I think I shall miss the trees mostly. Beautiful in all their seasons. Stark and spiky black in the winter. Harsh and shrill. Then lush and round and green in the summer. Lovely things. Year after year.' His eyes closed again, but his curled fingers continued to signify life. 'And to have known Shakespeare,' he said softly. '*And* Mozart.'

Constanza looked at Stallings and smiled, almost with wonder. The man knew he was dying and he was spending his last moments consciously recalling the beauties he had known in his life rather than the meanness or ugliness or misery that had to be there, too. He had gone through as many winters as summers and was choosing now to remember only the sun.

Constanza's feelings were becoming ambiguous, straddling both the tangible sadness of the occasion and, at the same time, an oddly dispassionate appreciation of the terrible beauty before him, a man dying in grace, someone who had lived his chosen life, lived it well, made (he liked to think) the very most of it and, in spite of the blip of violence done to him at the very end, was finishing up with the world's glories in his head and someone to hold his hand. How many people could say that? Worse, how many people could not.

For a while Constanza simply sat and tried to sort out unfamiliar feelings. He had had no practical experience in his life of holding a dying man's hand. Ultimately, and almost shockingly, one feeling came to dominate; he felt satisfied for the dying man. If the man himself couldn't say it, he, Constanza, would say it for him. It had been grand, just grand.

He looked up. Stallings's head had a different tilt to it, more towards the window. Constanza looked for what he knew he would not see, the pulsing vein, and felt for what he knew he would not feel, the responsive hand. Stallings was dead. Constanza sighed and looked out of the window; the tops of the trees were just turning orange in the sun's first light.

He withdrew his hand and, even as his eyes filmed over, he smiled. He had felt like this, exactly like this, only once before—when he had watched Sally give birth to their first daughter.

He found Starbuck at the nurse's station scribbling on a clipboard. 'He's dead,' Constanza said. 'Very quiet, very peaceful. Probably just what you had in mind.' Starbuck continued writing for a few seconds, then looked up. 'I passed the room a couple of times. Saw you chatting, holding his hand. That was very good of you. I don't know if it helped your case, but it helped mine—and certainly his.'

They regarded each other for an instant, sharing a moment that was much more intimate than just being in a hospital corridor at five-thirty in the morning. They had both, given the circumstances presented to them, properly and correctly helped a man into death.

'You believe in God?' suddenly blurted Constanza. His words astonished himself.

They evidently astonished Starbuck as well because for a few seconds he just stared. Then he smiled. 'No. I'm the worst kind of atheist.'

'Oh? What's that?'

'Jewish.'

Constanza smiled back, nodded. 'Right.' Then he frowned. 'Excuse me, but your name…'

'Yeah, Starbuck, I know. Throws a lot of people. Had mostly to do with an existentialist mother and ten days of unbridled passion on Cape Cod with a dashing Lieutenant-Commander. No big deal, really. Except maybe to me, right?'

'Uh, right,' said Constanza. 'Listen, is there anything I should do here now about this?'

'No, it's OK. From here on it's all my show. Incidentally, was he any help?'

'No,' said Constanza. 'Not at all.' He turned to go, then turned back. 'Listen, Starbuck, if you ever might need something, get into a situation where you might need some help or something, you could let me know, OK?'

Starbuck looked up, ready to smile, but seeing Constanza's face decided not to. 'Sure will, thanks. You never can tell, can you?'

# FIFTEEN

DAWSON ENTERED, took one look at Constanza, then sat down at his desk and activated the intercom. 'Mary,' he said softly, 'please do me a big favour and get a ham and egg sandwich from Frannie's... No, no, on a hard roll... No, no ketchup. It's for Phil... Yes, thanks very much.'

Constanza had a plastic coffee cup in his hand and was angrily striding up and down the length of Sam Dawson's office, four quick steps each way, then a savage turn. He seemed not to have heard Dawson, but suddenly, and without breaking stride, started talking to him. 'I mean, just how does a guy get this way?' He stopped, perched himself on the edge of the conference table and leaned forward intently. 'See, Sam, if it were a drunken brawl or a strungout hophead or a kid's panic during a hold-up, I could see it. But at bottom what we've got here is a well-thought-through, long-term plan covering at least several weeks, all in a relatively peaceful, intellectual setting, the end of which plan culminates in the guy personally sticking a knife into somebody's throat and personally ending her life. And then two days later he does it again, only this time it's with a club. And they're people he knows, right? Well, what gets me is how does he acquire the—the—sheer conceit to calmly do that, to decide that a life should end? Where does he get the psychological conviction that he has that right?' He stopped suddenly, voice angry and agitated, and looked directly at Dawson. 'I mean, just who the hell does he think he is?'

Christ, thought Dawson. First, Waterston, now his detective-sergeant. Well, Waterston he could excuse for taking some personal umbrage and briefly slipping his moorings, given all the circumstances. But Constanza? After nine years on the force? Even nine sheltered years should have been sufficient to give him more ballast than this.

Dawson nodded slowly and idly scratched his throat just under his chin where he hadn't shaved well. 'These your first deaths, Phil? Of any kind?'

Constanza nodded. 'Yeah, I guess. Is that it? Is it that simple, that obvious?'

'It might be,' said Dawson. 'Sounds like it to me. My own feeling is it speaks well for your sensibilities. Yes, Phil, he made somebody's life end. Caused it with his own hand. He really is one goddamned son of a bitch. Outrage is fine and I'm glad for you.' This time it was Dawson who leaned forward. Constanza drew back a bit. 'Now let me tell you something, Constanza. Your job isn't outrage. Waterston's might be, but not yours. Your job is to channel all your faculties into finding out who that guy is. You don't have the luxury of outrage—except once, to get it out of your system. You don't let anything interfere with your clearest and best thinking. You want to vent spleen? Vent it in your own time. Except you don't have any time of your own on this case so please stop indulging your sense of righteousness. We can't afford it. And besides, it'll interfere with your seriousness. You keep your emotional distance and your impersonalism. If you can't do that, you've got to let me know because we won't be doing our best work. And I'm not going to permit that, OK?'

Constanza pursed his lips, then slid off the desk and went back to his chair. He looked up at the lioness for a few moments, then back to Dawson. 'And you can turn it off that easily, Sam? You can shift gears from personal feeling to cold objectivity with the conscious turn of a dial? Here I go, switching now from disgust, horror and rage to cold, calculating observation and analysis.'

Dawson cocked an eye at Constanza 'You know your trouble, Phil? You're too white. Christ, you're not even Jewish—although, come to think of it, even the Jews I know your age aren't Jewish any more. This is the first spot of real, honest to goodness shit in your life, isn't it? Well, shit happens, Phil, just like the T-shirts say.' Dawson got up from behind his desk and came around to sit on the front of it. He smiled so that Constanza would know that while he, Dawson, was going to mean what he was going to say, he, Constanza, should be prepared for how he might be saying it. 'You've got to broaden your character, Phil. You've got to increase your dimensionality. Too much shelter is bad for growth, bad for maturity. And man, have you ever had shelter! I mean, Bergenfield High, Swarthmore, Turnpike Trooper, Kingsford detective. C'mon, fella. You've never been seriously rained on, and then have to punch in, have you? Well, the fact of the matter is, it's not all that hard. Phil, you're going to be amazed at how easy it is, how well you're going to do at it.'

Dawson stopped but continued to smile. Constanza remained silent and just looked at him. It was all true. He had led an antiseptic life, he thought to himself, and the consequent shortcomings were only to be expected. After a while Constanza nodded slightly and said, 'That's the second pep talk you've given me in two days, Sam.'

Dawson dropped his smile and turned serious. 'Hey, man, what are Chiefs of Police for?'

Constanza, admiring Dawson's use of his face, was again silent for a while. Then: 'You know what I think, Sam?'

Dawson kept his face mock-serious. 'What, Phil?'

'I think you may have outgrown your current job.'

Dawson kept his facial expression the same and remained silent.

Constanza dropped his smile, very conscious of how Dawson was keeping him off balance. 'Uh, one more thing,' he said, 'an objective thing. The fact that I don't seem to be able to get inside this guy's head, get any kind of a fix on him, is that a big drawback here?'

'No, Phil, it's not. You really don't have to get at his psyche to find out who he is. It's a mistake to think that a guy's particular warp on the ''why'' is always necessary, or even helpful, to discover the ''who'' and the ''what''. And that's really what we're all about. So save the analysis for later, and let's get on with it, OK?'

Constanza nodded several times, silently. 'Right, Sam. OK. Right.'

Mary Underwood suddenly knocked softly, entered, and without a word put a brown paper bag on the desk, turned, and left the room.

Dawson took a sandwich wrapped in wax paper from the bag and handed it to Constanza. 'Here, you probably haven't had any breakfast, yet.'

'That's all right, Sam. The coffee'll do just fine, honest.'

'No, coffee won't be enough. It'll just hop you up more. The protein and carbohydrate will do you good. Eat.' It'll also help bring you back to an even keel, he said to himself. It had been an odd five minutes, but Dawson, as usual, had kept the psychological initiative.

Constanza seemed to consider this, then took the sandwich and said, 'Yeah, you're probably right. I guess this has not been one of my more normal three hours.'

Dawson nodded. 'Get anything from Stallings before he died? Anything at all?'

'Nope. Not a thing. He had enough comprehension left to understand that he had been attacked because he knew something, only he couldn't come up with anything.' Constanza started taking large bites out of the sandwich. 'Say, this is pretty tasty.'

'Frannie makes a good breakfast. In fact, it's her best meal of the day.'

Constanza quickly finished the sandwich, then said, 'Excuse me, Sam, but can I use your john for a minute?'

'Sure, Phil.'

While Constanza was in the toilet Dawson called first the hospital and then the coroner to arrange for an autopsy on Stallings. Then he called Charlie Harris at the *Chronicle* to fill him in on Stallings's murder and to tell him that while it would duly be logged in on the police register he wouldn't be making any official public announcement of it until the evening's press conference. Dawson went on to give him Starbuck's name and to say that an autopsy would be made as soon as possible. Charlie Harris thanked him and said he owed him one.

Constanza came out of the toilet drying his hands. 'Look, Sam,' he said briskly, 'I want to talk to Thorndyke, the head of the library. I mean, right now. There are a couple of things that I want to know before I do any more thinking about this. Purely mechanical things, but they may be important. I know I scheduled in McCardle first thing in the morning, but this comes first now. I'll see

McCardle right afterwards, but I was wondering if meanwhile you could talk to the parents and see if they could give you any leads, specifically about Hilda Robertson's other boyfriend. How about we meet back here at around eleven-thirty. Is that all right with you?'

'That'll be fine, Phil. See you back here around eleven-thirty.'

As Constanza left, Dawson poured himself some coffee and asked Mary Underwood to get the Robertson home for him.

Dr Clement Thorndyke waved him in from the open doorway and motioned him to a seat opposite the room's most conspicuous object, a centrally positioned and superbly maintained Louis XV desk. The rest of the room looked like what Constanza was beginning to accept as the typical office of a ranking academic officer, namely an unprepossessing assemblage of nondescript furniture, most of whose surfaces were covered with books, papers, folders and manuscripts. Except, in this office, for the desk. It was Thorndyke's personal property inherited by his family through marriage several generations ago from a Huguenot émigré who had taken refuge in La Rochelle and then in England. Occasionally the desk proved to be an inconvenience, but Thorndyke had never even considered giving it up. Indeed, one of the conditions of his coming to Kingsford had been for the University to pay for its transport from Durham and then insure it for its catalogue value of $200,000. But Kingsford had wanted Thorndyke, and all the more when they found out that both Brown and Yale were also after him. He had a fine record of achievement, one that marked him for a step up in the academic hierarchy. In his ten years at Duke he had brought its library to 'world class' level (as he himself described it), to the point where important writers, mostly Southern but some Northern as well, were now leaving original manuscripts and notes there. In a kind of chicken-and-egg effect, this had both spawned and been fed by a veritable torrent of doctoral students, international conferences, visiting and exchange professorships and, not least, lots of public and private grant money. His worldwide network of personal and foundation contacts was legendary. Kingsford's final offer to him had been $7,000 higher than that of the closest competitor. And, of course, they had agreed to take care of his desk.

'No, no,' he was telling someone on the phone, 'I will not speak with his secretary, or with Professor Beal. I will speak only with Dr Furness... Yes, I understand that he is at a meeting and that you do not know how long he will be. Nevertheless, if he does not return the call by four this afternoon, he will lose his eight thousand dollar budget line. You may remind him that the fiscal year does end tomorrow and that he knew all this some time ago... Thank you.'

Thorndyke did not hang up the receiver but de-

pressed the activating button with a long forefinger
and looked across the room at Constanza. 'There's
one incoming call waiting. It will be brief. Then
I'm holding all calls so we can talk with no interruption. Will that be all right?'

Constanza nodded. Thorndyke thanked him and
lifted his finger from the telephone. 'Yes, Bernard... That's right, Bernard, no more middle-
aged, part-time housewives with Master's Degrees
in English who want to do something with their
afternoons. We already have nineteen in the system... I know we save money by being able to put
them on hourly wage but I don't want them to
dominate our service. We want to build up our
professionalism here... Well, then you'll just have
to tell her it's impossible. You'll recall we'd already discussed this last month... My dear man, I
don't care if she's President Waterston's wife, we
run Tavistock Library and this is our decision. You
may be as diplomatic as possible, but the bottom
line is no, and that's it... No, Bernard, there won't
be. The so-called union is a practising nonentity. I
have done more for the salary and working conditions of the staff of this library in the past five
years than their union has in fifteen. Now, please,
no more arguments, all right?... Right... Right.
Goodbye, then.'

Thorndyke hung up and addressed Constanza.
'So very sorry, Sergeant, ah, Constanza, is it?'

'Yes, Dr Thorndyke, Philip Constanza.'

'Right. We won't be interrupted now, until you

leave. I have already heard, just about twenty minutes ago, about poor Stallings. Please tell me how I can help in this dreadful business.'

Everything physical about Thorndyke was spare and long, arms, face, legs, ears, even hair. He wore no jacket and his movements were energetic and broad, so that much of his shirt-tail was already out of his trousers and his tie considerably off centre. Every so often, he would run bony fingers rapidly over his forehead. Constanza guessed that by three or four in the afternoon he would be quite dishevelled.

'Well, I was wondering, first, if you could tell me anything at all about that?'

'Sergeant, I can tell you at once that Professor Stallings was one of the best liked men at the University. He was a lovely man, simply a lovely man. Kind and gentle and considerate. And a magnificent scholar. Magnificent. I cannot possibly imagine anyone wanting to harm him. Except, of course, some madman who might want to silence him out of fear, or for something he might know. It *must* be something like that. Tell me, what do you think?'

Constanza already knew how fast news can travel in a small community, but he had never known that thinking, too, can travel that fast. 'Well, that's also our current thinking, and that leads me to a few questions. First, I'd like to know if Stallings had been using the library much this week. Any record of his being here, anyone seeing him.'

'Right,' said Thorndyke. 'Let me make a phone call or two.' He pulled at his chin for a few seconds, then thumbed through a circular file on his desk, jotting down several numbers. Then he turned to the telephone. After the first call he told Constanza that the same entrance guard had recognized Stallings entering the library both last night and the night before at around eight o'clock but had left without seeing him leave. 'We close down at ten, you know. This is actually quite typical for him. I happen to know that one of Stallings's habits was to start his library work in the evening and often work until midnight or so. A habit of old age, I'm told.'

'Would others know of this habit, also?'

'Oh, I'm sure they would. He's been doing it for years and he was very visible.'

Thorndyke made a second call and after hanging up informed Constanza that Stallings had checked out books three days ago and also two days ago. 'That would make it Monday and Tuesday,' he said, 'but I'm afraid I cannot tell you what time of day.'

'Tell me,' said Constanza, 'what the Sunday situation is.'

'Sunday,' said Thorndyke, 'is exactly like any other day, except that we begin operations at noon instead of eight-thirty and shut down at eight instead of ten.'

'And if one wanted to return books?'

'One either drops them off at the circulation desk where a clerk checks them in immediately, or, when the circulation desk is not being manned, deposits them into a book drop and they are checked in and reshelved the following morning.'

'So that about how long after the book's return are they reshelved?'

'No more than half a day.'

'Dr Thorndyke, it may be important for me to know if Stallings was in the library this past Sunday. Can you help me on that?'

'We'll see.' He reached for the phone again. 'Hillary, do you have the schedule of personnel on lobby duty at the library this past Sunday?... Right. Please get hold of it, contact the people and...yes, including the students, and ask them if anyone had seen Professor Stallings at any time during Sunday... Right... Yes, well, please stop that and start on this immediately and let me know the instant you get anything positive... Thank you very much.' He hung up and turned to Constanza. 'As soon as I hear anything I shall, of course, let you know, although it may be a couple of hours.'

For a moment Constanza considered asking Thorndyke to keep these inquiries confidential, but then decided against it. It would really be almost impossible by now. Judging from the astonishing speed with which news seemed to travel in Kingsford, almost everyone would soon know from the telephone calls of the last half-hour that he was tracing Stalling's movements over the past few days. Then it occurred to Constanza that, in fact, there might be a plus in having it made public. If it reached the killer, it might exert some pressure on him. It might induce some reaction from him, perhaps provoke him into doing something, something aberrant that would stand out against the background of his normal behaviour.

'Look, Professor, I think I'd prefer that our talk here not be kept secret. In fact, I wouldn't at all mind if it were to be made public, without putting a strain on it, though. You know what I mean?'

'Right,' said Thorndyke. 'I think I understand. So if it reaches the killer, he'll have something to think about, perhaps goad him into something that might help identify him, right?'

Christ, was it that transparent? Were all his clever thoughts and insights so damned obvious? Or was it that everybody around here was so much sharper than what he had become accustomed to in his usual dealings with people?

'Professor, is there anything else that you can tell us that might be helpful, something that I'm not asking about because of my ignorance?'

Thorndyke shook his head slowly. 'Not that I can think of, I'm afraid. If I do, I'll certainly give you a call.'

'Then let me thank you for your time, sir.'

'Not at all. And good luck, Sergeant.'

# SIXTEEN

ALTHOUGH IT WOULD ordinarily take him only five minutes to cycle from Thorndyke's office to McCardle's Pancakes, Constanza made his ride along the route he knew so well a more leisurely ten. First he chewed on the fact that while he now knew how the murderer would know pretty much where and when to find Stallings, he still had no idea of why he was killed. And second, towards the end of his ride he chewed on exactly what he could reasonably expect Ted McCardle to tell him about this case.

He left the campus at the eighty-year-old pink dogwood tree that shaded the main guard house, carefully walked his bike across University Street to where the shops were, and locked it up at the rack in front of McCardle's Pancakes. McCardle had originally wanted the sign to read 'Pancakes and Burgers', but the Planning Council had considered 'Burgers' to be out of character with the tone they wanted to maintain. 'Pancakes' evidently was acceptable.

Five minutes later they were in McCardle's upstairs office, sipping coffee. The office fronted on University Street and had a splendid view of the campus behind the length of well-tended fieldstone wall that separated this part of the University from the street. Constanza had never been in the upstairs of any of these buildings lining University Street across from the University and was disappointed to see that, at least in this one, dilapidation had clearly set in. The window-sills were visibly warped and some of the floorboards had begun to separate. The aluminium paint on both the steam radiators was peeling and a section of filigreed ceiling moulding was missing. The general air of interior shabbiness was very much at odds with the exterior that faced the street and was maintained in spanking new condition, the mock-Tudor beams freshly painted, the off-white stucco sparkling clean, the tasteful sign carefully aligned with its neighbours for a pleasing visual effect. Constanza did know that the Planning Council had zoned the whole of University Street for two storeys, and had veto power over the appearance of the shop signs.

'Thanks for seeing me, Mr McCardle.'

'Not at all, Sergeant Constanza. I'm presuming you're looking into the, uh, deaths over at the University.'

Constanza smiled. 'Having trouble with certain words, McCardle?'

Ted McCardle smiled back. 'Yeah, right. Sorry. I'm presuming you're investigating the library murders with a view to determining who the murderer is.'

'Much better. More in keeping with your background.'

McCardle raised his eyebrows. 'Which is?'

'Ph.D. in Solid-State Chemistry from Lehigh, seven years at DuPont, two at the Wharton Business School. Then buying Sal's Luncheonette and in two years turning it into the students' semi-official burger and pancake place.'

'Not semi-official. Official. You investigating me, too?'

'No investigation necessary. There's an element in this town where people like you, with your background, doing what you've done, well, you get talked about. Eventually, the town's detective-sergeant will hear about it. No big deal.'

'And the detective-sergeant, with his background, he gets talked about, too. But no big deal there, either. Must be the town, right?'

'Right. Incidentally, this is terrific coffee. Marvellous flavour but without any sharp acid taste. No wonder the kids come here.'

'The kids don't drink this. You can't charge three dollars a cup in an operation like this and get away with it, and anything less would lose me money on this coffee. It costs me twenty dollars a pound at a little place on East Seventy-Third Street in New York.'

Constanza pointed to a bed in a corner of the room away from the windows. 'Do you live here, too?'

'No. I bunk out here occasionally on a late Saturday night when I have to open up early for Sunday. Also, I sometimes could use a nap around four in the afternoon. Also, I sometimes bring a girl—a consenting, legal adult—up here. I actually live out on Carriage Hill Road.'

'Pretty fancy,' said Constanza.

'I can afford it,' said McCardle.

'Tell me,' said Constanza, 'did Hilda Robertson ever come in here?'

'Yes, pretty often as a matter of fact. A lot of the kids do, and even some faculty. And, yes, I get to know a lot of them by name. I circulate, sit at tables, talk. Part of my image—good for business. And sometimes I even care. You'd be surprised how many kids will talk to the sympathetic burger man closer to their own age rather than to their parents.'

'Maybe I wouldn't be so surprised,' said Constanza.

'No, maybe not. Not with a Master's in sociology.'

Constanza smiled and nodded. 'McCardle, I hear Hilda Robertson had a boyfriend other than Professor Beecham. Is that true?'

The question conveyed a lot and both of them knew it. It conveyed that Constanza knew about Beecham and Robertson, that he assumed that McCardle knew it, that he actually *knew* and hadn't just heard about the other boyfriend, that he was here because McCardle was a repository of a small town's gossip and fact—and, finally, that Constanza was expecting hard information.

McCardle hesitated, then said, 'I'm hesitating only because I want to be sure of the quality of the information I'm going to give you. I'd prefer not to skew it, OK? I'd like to see the guy get caught, too.'

'Fine with me,' said Constanza.

'Hilda Robertson would come in here occasionally with a guy named Neil Washington. History major. Athletic scholarship. Middle twenties. Nice-looking. Black, or what they used to call light coloured. Never for dinner, mostly for lunch, but some breakfasts, too. No attempt to hide anything. Almost certainly sleeping together, but not a real heavy thing, no real regularity, you know? Social sleeping, the kids call it, with everybody careful, physically and emotionally. Probably mimicking the "social drinking" of their parents. Anyway, they were a likeable couple and seemed to fit in well. He actually came in here yesterday and the place quietened down a bit when he was recognized. Couple of kids came up to tell him they were sorry. He lives off campus, just outside Trenton, so as to avoid the boarding fees. The University lets him do that because of economic hardship. I don't have his address, but I presume you can get that from some office across the street.' McCardle paused, thought a bit, then shrugged. 'I think that's about all I've got by way of hard fact, Sergeant.'

In his rush out of the house that morning Constanza had forgotten to take his tape-recorder, and so had been writing furiously in his notebook. He finished and looked up. 'Doing just fine, McCardle, just fine. Now, getting past the hard facts and on to the level of, ah, personal skew, do you have anything that you think might bear on all of this?'

McCardle walked to the coffee machine and poured both of them another cup. 'Right,' he said, 'strongly personal, OK?'

'Please,' said Constanza.

'Well, I'll tell you. For a gal who's supposed to be the official shack-up of her Department chairman who has just given her a big personal push, she seemed awfully comfortable and at ease going around with her other boyfriend. Granted, I'm about half a generation removed from most of these kids, so I may be a little out of touch with their social mores, but even so it seems they were a little cavalier about themselves, knowing the circumstances. I can't tell you exactly why, but it seemed to me out of character for Washington to be so comfortable with the situation. I recall her as being pretty lively, but he comes across as somewhat conservative. Again, can't tell exactly why, but...'

'Are you talking here about the conservatism of the not yet secure upwardly mobile?'

McCardle smiled broadly. 'Very good, Sergeant. Very well expressed. You must have taken a course.'

Constanza grinned. 'You do seem to be talking about a delicate situation.'

'Well, you did ask for a personal slant.'

'Yes, I certainly did. Anything else? Anything at all?'

'No, nothing more, I'm afraid. The other principals in the case—that is, so far as I know them—don't come here. Beecham, his wife, other guys in Art. And poor old Stallings.'

'Any other people you think might be, ought to be, principals? Take your time on this.'

McCardle shook his head slowly, paused to think, then shook it again. 'No, really not. I think I've told you all I know that bears on this. It's a real shitty business, Sergeant. Let me know if I can ever do anything to help, OK?'

Constanza wrote again in his notebook, then looked up and nodded. 'Well, thanks very much. You've given us a lot of stuff and I appreciate it.'

'Any time, Sergeant.' He smiled. 'You know, I don't seem to see you downstairs. The food really isn't all that bad. Drop in some time.'

Constanza smiled back, apologetically, he hoped. 'I'm a little bit of a food nut. Too much beef fat, pancake syrup and ice-cream downstairs for me. But if you ever start serving that coffee downstairs, I'll take you up on that and even bring my wife.'

McCardle shook his head. 'Afraid that'll never

happen. Here, let me walk you out. Seeing me talking with Kingsford's detective force will be a boost for McCardle's image.'

# SEVENTEEN

IT WAS THE TAIL END of the lunch-hour, so there were a few empty tables in the middle of the floor. Dawson and Constanza walked past these, most of which still held the remains of pizzas, and headed for a far corner where a booth was just being cleared.

'You ever been here before?' asked Constanza.

'As a matter of fact, no,' said Dawson.

'There's another DiLorenzo's in Chambersburg, but it's not the same as this. That's the one the kids go to. This is a different place. More serious.' They both smiled.

Dawson looked around as he reached for a menu card, and saw immediately that Constanza meant it. There was no juke-box here, and although the décor was still dominated by luncheonette-style formica-and-chrome, an ambience of some formality was clearly present. While waiters still looked like late teenagers, they spoke softly, wore short-sleeved white shirts and two of them wore black bow ties. And the clientele seemed distinctly older than that of the usual pizza place; several of the girls were in skirts and blouses, while some of their male companions wore jackets and ties. These were quiet office people, some of whom had driven over from the State Capitol complex.

Moving among the tables in deliberate, almost stately motion, was a tall, portly man with a good head of straight, jet-black hair just beginning to show an occasional grey smear. A light sheen of moisture covered a face dominated by a nose outlined in two bold, slashing strokes that could have come directly from an ancient Roman coin. The young waiters called him either Mr DiLorenzo or 'sir'.

There was nothing but pizza and soft drinks on the menu. 'What flavours do you like, Sam?' asked Constanza.

'You're the connoisseur here, Phil. Why don't you decide for us?'

'Well, I know you like spicy stuff, but sometimes that doesn't agree with me too well. How about we order one large, half extra cheese, other half sausage and mushrooms. I think those are the best, anyhow. OK with you?'

'Sure, fine. What we don't finish, we can take home, right?'

'Oh, we'll finish it all right.'

After the order had been placed and utensils laid at their table they began softly to discuss the morning's events.

'Did Thorndyke say anything else in his message,' asked Constanza, 'besides the fact that Stallings was definitely seen in the library last Sunday night?'

'No,' said Dawson, 'just that one short message.'

Constanza nodded and said, 'OK. So now we've got Stallings in the library every night this week including Sunday, and from what we know that's not at all unusual. I've been thinking about something on the way down here, Sam, and I want you to give me a couple of minutes on this.' Constanza began absently rotating his fork on the table. 'Listen. Robertson is killed late Monday night. Stallings is killed on Wednesday night. He's killed because he knows something. Turns out he doesn't realize he knows it. Also turns out he's in the library Tuesday night, doing what almost everybody knows is his usual thing. My question is, why wasn't he killed last Tuesday night? Why does the killer, who thinks that what Stallings knows is dangerous enough to kill for, wait two whole days until Wednesday night to kill him? After all, he had a perfectly good opportunity Tuesday night. He knew where he was and when he would be there. I mean, it was just like Sunday, Monday and Wednesday—when he did kill him—right?'

Dawson wasn't sure if he was supposed to join in, if only to play straight man, or not to say anything and play silent sounding-board. He compromised by nodding and then reaching into a brown paper bag on the seat beside him to withdraw two cans of beer. He yanked open the aluminium tabs on both, kept one for himself and set one down on the table in front of Constanza. An observant waiter brought over two empty glasses from across the room.

'He didn't kill him until Wednesday,' continued Constanza, 'because he didn't know, or realize, until Wednesday that Stallings had information worth killing for. Now, there are two possibilities.' He stopped while a waiter put a steaming aromatic wheel of pizza down before them and with swift motions cut it into ten slices. Dawson and Constanza both slid slices of each of the toppings they had ordered on to their plates and began eating rapidly. Constanza went on as though uninterrupted. 'Either Stallings didn't acquire the information until Wednesday or he had it all along, again without knowing it, and the killer didn't realize it until Wednesday. Actually it isn't all that important, because it turned out that Stallings never realized it. The important point is that the *killer* didn't realize it until Wednesday. If he had realized it earlier, like on Tuesday, he would have killed him earlier. What happened on Wednesday that triggered the killer's decision? That's the crucial thing as far as Stallings's killing is concerned.'

Dawson felt he had to interrupt. 'Maybe nothing specific happened on Wednesday. Maybe it just came out of the blue. That happens a lot, too, Phil.'

'Yes, Sam, but that line of reasoning won't help us.'

Dawson slipped another slice of pizza off its large aluminium tray on to his plate. 'I've been following you pretty well up to now, Phil, but that last remark is throwing me.'

'Look, Sam, I once had an intern friend who told me that doctors are taught that if there are two things you can diagnose equally well, and one of them you can't do anything about and the other one you can, you always diagnose the thing you can help.'

'Hold on a minute,' said Dawson. 'You telling me that you know something that came to light on Wednesday that would provoke Stallings's murder?'

'No. I'm only saying that something did, Sam. Unfortunately, I don't know what it is. If I did, I think I would have this case solved.'

Dawson nodded. 'OK, I've got it now.' He munched his way idly through the pizza slice. 'Well, it all sounds a little tenuous to me, but it's a good thought, the kind of thing that you might be wanting to keep in mind without its driving you too fast to any concrete conclusions.' He looked up suddenly, gesturing with the pizza in his hand. 'You know, these go down pretty easy. I think this is number four for me. How about you?'

'Yeah, same for me. I told you we'd finish it. They're different here. Lighter, with a thinner, flakier crust. But plenty enough to chew on, right? And everything seems to taste cleaner, with a less metallic aftertaste, right?'

'Right, Phil, right. But before you start discuss-

ing the vintage on this pizza let's talk about Neil
Washington. How did he sound on the phone?'

'As a matter of fact, real subdued, as though
either very down or very preoccupied. I guess
that's understandable, given the circumstances. I
wasn't specific about what we were going to talk
about, only that it would be about the murder. Neither of us brought up the topic of a lawyer during
the questioning so I'm presuming there won't be
any. If he insists when we get there, what do we
do?'

'I never predict about that. Depends on tone,
feel, vibrations—stuff like that. We'll see.'

They each finished their fifth slice quickly and
Constanza called for the check. DiLorenzo himself
brought it over and asked if everything was all
right.

'Just fine,' said Constanza. 'Incidentally, this is
Mr Dawson. Friend of mine. First time for him.'
DiLorenzo shook hands with Dawson. 'Hope you
enjoyed your pizza,' he said, 'and that we see you
again.'

'Yes, I did and you certainly will.' Dawson, taking his cue from the other two, spoke almost sol-
emnly. Then he brought up the remaining four cans
of beer in the six-pack at his side and offered them
to DiLorenzo. 'Please, when things quieten down
we'd like you to give these to the boys in the
kitchen if that's all right with you.'

For the first and only time during their lunch,

they saw DiLorenzo smile. 'That's very kind of you. Thank you.'

They paid the bill, left the pizzeria, and as they got into the car and drove off, Dawson said, 'Christ, were you ever right, Phil. That is one serious pizza place. Oh, by the way, before I forget, I found the Robertsons at home and had a long chat with them over the phone. Seems that their daughter was almost never home, and they knew essentially nothing about her life at the University. They admitted, in fact, that they were quite distant, a generational thing they called it. They knew none of her friends, had no letters from her, had different politics. Very often she didn't show up for holidays. Last few years didn't even see much of her during summer recess. Absolutely nothing helpful. And, of course, they had never heard the name of Neil Washington.'

THEY DROVE along Hamilton Avenue towards the centre of Trenton. Dawson was directing Constanza, telling him first to make a right turn on to Broad Street and, after a few blocks, a left. Neil Washington lived on a quiet street of almost identical two-storeyed row houses. They didn't see many people but those they did see were black. They had taken one of the two unmarked police cars, but Dawson said that it really wouldn't help. Any knowledgeable person in a neighbourhood like this seeing a pair of men, one black, one white, stop and enter a house would know that they were cops. 'No help for it,' he had said.

Their ring was quickly answered by a tall, well-muscled boy in chinos and a polo shirt. Constanza judged that the muscles and the height would make him either power forward on varsity basketball or wide receiver on football. A pronounced loping stride suggested basketball. The regular-featured, nondescript face was serious, almost sad. 'Hello, I'm Neil Washington,' he said. 'You're the police officers, right?'

Dawson and Constanza identified themselves, told him they did not have a warrant, said they would like to speak with him about Hilda Robertson and asked if he would like a lawyer. Neil Washington picked nervously at his fingernails and seemed tense, but nevertheless managed a weak smile and asked if he needed one. 'Not really,' said Dawson, 'but we're supposed to go through all that. Actually, only a matter of form.'

He led them down a darkened hallway, body swaying slightly from side to side with each long stride, and directly into a large bright kitchen whose pronounced tidiness and cleanliness practically compelled attention. Both Dawson and Constanza recognized it as one of the hallmarks of the transitional black family, indeed of any immigrant family, just entering the middle class. Their knowledge had come from different sources, however, Constanza's from the classroom, Dawson's from the warrens of black North Philadelphia.

'The kitchen is actually the nicest and most comfortable room in the house,' said Washington as he pulled out some chairs from around the table. Even his hospitality was unsmiling.

'It usually is,' said Dawson. 'At least, when I was growing up.' Damn. He immediately regretted saying it because even as he heard himself, he knew it sounded patronizing. 'Look, Mr Washington, you know why we're here and what we're trying to do...' Good Christ, couldn't he say anything right? 'Anyway, Sergeant Constanza here is carrying the brunt of the investigation so if you don't mind he'd like to ask some questions.'

Neil Washington hesitated when Constanza took the tape-recorder out of his bag, but only for an instant, and quickly said that no, he wouldn't mind. Nevertheless, Constanza put it on the floor, out of sight.

For the first few minutes Constanza simply tried to get Washington to relax a bit and asked about his general situation. He quickly learned that the Washingtons owned their house, courtesy of a second mortgage, occupied the ground floor and rented the upper floor at minimal rent to a husbandless cousin on welfare with two girls aged seven and nine. Washington's father sorted mail at the Post Office, mother clerked at the Motor Vehicle Bureau, and sister attended Mercer County Community College. The upstairs family were all at school, the girls at grade school, the mother trying to get enough credits for a high school diploma under a special adult school programme. Neil Washington was at Kingsford University on an athletic scholarship. Basketball.

'Mr Washington, how well did you know Hilda Robertson?'

Washington nodded and his face took on an air of resignation, as though an expectation had been fulfilled. He began picking at his fingernails again. Then he sighed and looked up. 'I think I'd like to say a couple of things on that, if that's OK.' He spoke almost forlornly.

'Please,' said Constanza. He was wondering why he and Dawson were being so polite and soft spoken, almost hushed. For himself, it was partly because Washington's manner was already showing some ineffable sense of loss. And, of course, he was black.

'First, I want you to know that I'll do anything to help find the bastard who killed her. I, uh, liked Hilda Robertson. Liked her very much. And, well, she liked me, too. She really did. We went around a little. We, uh… Listen, I know I may seem nervous about all this. Well, I am nervous. I'm not used to having discussions with cops. This is my first one, and it's making me a little tense, you know?'

And, thought Constanza to himself, you grew up learning that cops, like telegrams, were harbingers of bad things, things to be avoided, things that usually involved someone's troubles, maybe even your own. And, in general, you were right.

'Sure, we understand. It's just that we have to get as much information about this thing as we can and, well, you were going around with her, right? Tell, me, Mr Washington, just for the record, can you account for your whereabouts last night and Monday night?'

'Yesterday yes, Monday no. Yesterday I was here at home. Monday, I had been studying all day and went to a late movie here in town to clear my head. I was alone, though.'

'Do you do that often?'

'No, but it's exam time now and it works for me.'

'Mr Washington, could you please tell us to, uh, what level your relationship with Miss Robertson had progressed? Perhaps I should tell you that we will, of course, be speaking with other people about this. You know, friends, colleagues, people like that. Already have, to some degree. It's all in our line of work, so to speak.' Constanza was keeping his tone of voice as noncommittal as possible.

Washington rose, went to the sink and poured himself a glass of water from the faucet. 'Would you people like anything?' he asked.

Both Dawson and Constanza declined.

Washington returned to the table and sat down. 'We were sleeping together. Have been for a couple of months.' His mouth twitched. 'Had been, I guess, now.'

'Did it start before or after her involvement with Beecham?' asked Constanza expressionlessly.

'After,' said Washington. 'It really all happened very fast. About three days is all it took. Like I said, we really liked each other.' He finished the water and moved the empty glass around on the table. He looked up suddenly. 'Listen, does my family have to know about this? Do they have to be told? They didn't know about any of this, about my sleeping or even dating a white girl. Or even knowing a girl who was murdered. They wouldn't know what to make of it, but I know it would bother them, bother them a lot. They're a little, uh, old-fashioned about things like this and I wouldn't like to hurt them, you know? Does it have to come out?'

'All these conversations are strictly confidential,' said Constanza, 'and the facts in them are only made public when absolutely necessary, like when trying to catch or convict a murderer.' Washington nodded.

'Can you think of anyone,' asked Constanza, 'who had it in for Hilda Robertson to a degree that might lead to murder? I mean, Beecham had a wife. He had a daughter at Johns Hopkins. There were professional colleagues, especially young ones, who might have been incensed over blatantly obvious favouritism. There might be former girl-friends of Beecham's around, or for that matter boyfriends of Miss Robertson. Know anything about any possibilities there? Any situations we should know about?'

Washington frowned and slowly shook his head. 'No, not that I can think of. I mean, there was the occasional cup of coffee with someone, but nothing serious.'

'Like you, Mr Washington?'

'Right. Like me. And Beecham.'

Dawson spoke for the first time since Constanza had started his questioning. 'Son, was sex a big part of it between you and Miss Robertson? I mean, a real big part?'

Washington stared at the empty glass before him, then simply nodded. But he quickly raised his head and continued. 'But it was more than just that. It really was—' Washington suddenly stopped as though even he recognized the triteness of what he was about to say. His voice trailed away leaving silence for a moment.

Constanza waited a decent interval, then continued. 'Tell me, did Miss Robertson ever say anything that would suggest that Beecham was a particularly jealous man? Suppose Beecham is a guy who finally discovers his mistress is sleeping with someone else.' He remembered McCardle's last remark. 'I mean, you were going around pretty publicly with Hilda Robertson. Movies, lunch, coffee in the student centre and even breakfast at McCardle's. It was pretty common knowledge about Beecham and Robertson. Look at it from our point of view. Wouldn't it strike you as odd that, given all the circumstances, you would practically flaunt your relationship with the Robertson girl?'

Washington rose, refilled his glass with water, and walked slowly back to the table.

Dawson spoke again. 'Son, lying now would almost certainly do you more harm than good. Much more harm. You got an awful lot to lose if you start screwing around with us, and what with the complexities of the situation here, I really don't think you'd be able to pull it off. Honest.'

Constanza glanced at Dawson and saw his hand, out of sight from Washington, move downward in a 'cool it' gesture.

Everyone was quiet now. Washington looked first at Dawson, then at Constanza. Then he cleared his throat. 'One night about a month ago she got a little high at a party and I drove her home. She…well, we started to fool around and I guess I showed some resentment about her situation with Beecham. Pretty dumb of me, I suppose. Then she laughed and said she would tell me about him.' Washington took a mouthful of water, swallowed it and took a deep breath. 'She told me that Professor Beecham was bisexual. He could, and did, go either way. She said she was partly his cover, his evidence for being straight. She was also, ultimately, supposed to supply the reason for his divorce, which he wanted very much. His promoting her was part payment for agreeing to the situation, part consistency with the cover, and part payment for, uh, sleeping with him.' He stopped and licked his lips. 'She also said she liked making it with him, that he was, you know, real good in the sack.' He cleared his throat again. 'Said she got an extra charge from knowing about him, about how he was. She said she liked it with me, too, but in a different way, because there was more feeling, a different feeling, with me. In time, she said, everything would all die down and nobody would be the wiser. She told me not to worry, not to be concerned, nothing to feel guilty about, just to enjoy ourselves. And we really did. We…she was really very…I mean, I had never known anybody like her, you know?' He drank a lot of the water. 'Well, that's it. I don't know if you knew any of this, but that's it. That's the truth. There wouldn't be any sense in her making up anything like that, would there? As for our going around, well, that's the way she wanted it. Said she didn't want to feel controlled by her situation with Beecham. And I guess I just went along with whatever she wanted. It was that strong. For me, anyhow.'

Everyone was motionless. Constanza's mouth was open. Dawson was frowning. Washington continued to look at the table. After a time Constanza shifted his feet and said, 'I see. Right. Tell me, did you ever speak with Beecham, get to know him at all?'

'No, never met him. I think if you weren't in Art you wouldn't even take a course with him. It's not like music or psych where some low-level course is a pre-req for a general degree.'

'Mr Washington, can you think of any reason why Alardyce Stallings would be murdered by the same man who killed Miss Robertson? Can you think of any connection between the two?'

'You know, I've been thinking about that ever since you called earlier, and I just can't come up with anything. Not a damn thing. Except that Stallings might have known something and had to be silenced.'

Constanza nodded and turned to Dawson. Dawson shrugged and shook his head. Constanza reached down and turned off the tape-recorder. 'Well,' he said, 'I guess that's all, then. You've been very cooperative and helpful. It was good of you to see us. Oh, by the way, please let us know if you're planning to leave town, OK?'

They turned to leave, Washington leading the way. As they were going out the front door, Dawson turned back to face Washington. 'You did the right thing back there, giving us that information. Exactly the right thing. And we'll make certain that the talk we had goes no further unless absolutely necessary. Thank you, Mr Washington, and best of luck to you.'

They left and again Dawson drove. For several blocks neither of them spoke. Finally, Dawson said, 'We're definitely past surprise here, Phil, and clearly approaching weird. You make anything at all out of this?'

'Not a thing, Sam. If anything, I see it as a further complication, like a jagged piece to fit into a jigsaw puzzle when all the open spaces are smooth. Know what I mean?'

'Yeah, I know what you mean,' said Dawson.

'Sam, listen, are we going right back into Kingsford?'

'I was planning to, yes. You got anything in mind?'

'Well, what I'd like to do now is check Stallings's movements back to last Sunday if I can, because that's when I think the events leading to the actual murders began. You know, the return of the Caravaggio books. I know he lived alone in a small house on Squire Road, and maybe his neighbours can help me out. We know where he spent his evenings this week, but I want to know where he went and especially whom he saw during the day. See, I have the strong feeling that following up on Stallings's killing, using that one as the starting-point, might actually be more fruitful right now. I don't think there was any long-term planning for that one, so maybe there's more chance of a slip-up there, or of finding some overt connection between the two.'

'You going to begin as soon as we get back?'

'Yes, I want to pick up a car, maybe get some of the guys to help out on legwork and start right in. That OK with you?'

'Fine. As a matter of fact I was going to ask you not to be at this evening's press conference. It may be rough and if only one of us, namely me, is there, it'll be easier to put spin on it.'

'How do you mean, rough?'

'Well, they're going to go after Stallings's murder, and they may begin to play hardball with questions about serial killings, a small-town force biting off more than it can chew, sacrificing effective investigation in the interest of exercising more hands-on control, shit like that.'

Again they rode in silence for a while. Then Constanza spoke. 'You think they may be right on that, Sam?'

Dawson took his time, then shook his head. 'No. Not yet, anyhow. I really don't think that a lot more people asking a lot more questions would produce more progress. But that could change in a couple of days. It may have to be considered. We'll see. Meanwhile this press conference is one case where only one guy handling an audience would be better than two. I'll say you're too busy pursuing promising leads. Again.'

# EIGHTEEN

CONSTANZA DISCOVERED two things about Stallings's daily life during his questioning of neighbours and friends that day. One was that he took a nap in the afternoon, generally between two o'clock and four, and the other was that he maintained an office at the University where he customarily worked between the hours of nine a.m. and noon.

He used Stallings's key to get into his cottage. Walking up the driveway, he idly picked up two issues of the *Chronicle,* each neatly folded for easy tossing and brought them into the house. He read the dates on them. Today and yesterday. He sighed and made a mental note not only to cancel the newspaper deliveries but also to contact the utilities and telephone people. As far as he knew, there was nobody connected with Stallings who would do that and Constanza, as a public servant, thought it duly appropriate that he should.

The house was neat and trim, the only anachronism visible being two candy bars on an otherwise bare run of counter space in the kitchen. The beds in both bedrooms were made, the magazines on the sitting-room coffee table were tidily stacked, the venetian blinds were of uniform length. His admittedly superficial examination (he found it psychologically difficult to disturb things) yielded nothing of interest until he entered the study, where he struck gold in the form of an appointments calendar laid out smack in the middle of the desk. There, as befitted a tidy British academic in his late seventies, in the neatest of handwriting were the people he had been scheduled to see and the places to go for the entire week, and even the preceding week. It was exactly what he had hoped to find.

He saw two entries each for today and tomorrow. No, he thought ruefully, the dry cleaning would not, after all, be picked up today and he would not be having lunch with Miss Chisholm on Friday nor going to see *Brief Encounter* with her at the University's annual film festival.

Constanza listed the people named on Stallings's calendar for the previous five days, and quickly determined that they all were in either the University directory or the local telephone book. He was about to start right in calling them for appointments when a growling stomach made him look at his wristwatch. Christ, it was eight forty-five.

It was as good a time as any to stop for a moment and catch up on some mundane, daily routines like eating and calling his wife. And, anyhow, maybe he shouldn't just start calling a bunch of people without thinking a bit more about it. And he might as well do that over some supper.

First, he called Sally and told her he was OK but that she should put what dinner she might be saving for him in the fridge and not wait up for him. He would grab something to eat and he really didn't know when he would be home. Sally calmly said to take care and Constanza said not to worry, he would. This was not the first time he had phoned in with a message like this, and he knew that when he did get home he would probably find meat and vegetables neatly arranged on a platter, all carefully covered with plastic and ready for the microwave.

Then he called Dawson, first at home and then, after no answer, at the office, where he found him. 'Sam? Phil. I'm at Stallings's house. How'd the conference go?'

'Bad, Phil, really bad. The news about Stallings was out, of course, and they started right in about inside jobs and insufficient resources and inexperienced people and keeping things under wraps and everything else you could think of. Even Charlie Harris joined in. I did the best I could, saying we had some promising leads, but in the end I had to say that yes, we were of course considering calling in outside help from either Philadelphia or Trenton; that our first consideration had always been, and would continue to be, the best possible investigation. Stallings's killing is going to force our hand here, I'm afraid. Unless we get a real breakthrough in the next couple of days I think I'm going to have to do something along those lines. I filled them in on some details and the conference ended only a half-hour ago. Oh, by the way, I didn't mention Neil Washington or, needless to say, the information he gave us. To tell the truth, I actually forgot but nobody seemed to have tumbled to him yet. You got anything on your end?'

Constanza told him about Stallings's appointments calendar. 'Following on what you just told me, suppose I get Cannetti, Howard and Frederick to do some interrogating tomorrow morning along with myself. With any luck we ought to get through the list by midday. Then, sometime before the weekend, let's sit down and see what we've got.'

'Sounds good,' said Dawson. 'I like your choice of names, even if Frederick is only a patrolman. Keep in touch. I'll be here most of the day tomorrow, and if not here, Mary will know where I am.'

They said goodbye. Constanza called the three officers he had mentioned to Dawson, found them all at home, and told them to drop their scheduled routines for tomorrow and meet with him at eleven-thirty. The duty sergeant would rearrange personnel schedules. He told them what they would be doing, and that they would be getting details in the morning.

Constanza left Stallings's house and drove to a small Chinese restaurant he knew in a nearby mall rather than to Kingsford centre to get some dinner. He wanted to minimize the chance of running into any reporters and having to answer questions. He chose a table in a far corner, ordered chicken with broccoli, sipped his green tea and thought.

There were large chunks of it laid out now and in view of Dawson's report Constanza decided to begin replacing absolute fact with highly likely fact. Robertson's murder was the planned one, the one that the killer really wanted and spent many days, weeks even, setting up. The mechanism for that one was known, with the murderer setting up the time and place in the library. Then came Stallings's murder, unplanned and hasty, though again in the library, and the unknown information for the suppression of which he had been killed. Next, in rapid order, came the other boyfriend and Hilda Robertson's peculiar arrangement with a bisexual Beecham. Motives and lack of alibi were rampant, although jealousy of one sort or another still seemed the likely heart of everything. The chunks were there all right, what was missing was any network of linkage among them that would indicate a strong suspect.

A waiter set an attractive platter before him, emerald green broccoli and white chicken sitting in a dark brown sauce, along with a sparkling bowl of rice. The smell of ginger root was strong. Constanza's salivary glands flooded his mouth but, following his habit, he ate a half dozen forkfuls of rice before starting in on the chicken.

The more he thought about it, the more he became convinced that Stallings's killing held the crucial clue to it all. It would, in the end, all flow from that. That murder was a desperate, unforeseen act. Everything pointed to it. In planning, method and timing, it was the polar opposite of the Robertson murder. The fact that the killer had decided that Stallings had to die to keep his knowledge secret meant to Constanza that that knowledge pointed directly at him. Well, that didn't require any great deductive powers. But maybe following Stallings's path and looking at his activities over the past several days would help. At least, that was the general idea he would give his people tomorrow morning before they started out.

He finished the platter of chicken and found that he still wasn't satisfied. He must have been hungrier than he thought. He decided to indulge himself and ordered fried bananas for dessert and another pot of tea.

It was eleven-fifteen before he got home and found himself dog-tired. Well, Christ, it had been one hell of a long day. Sally had left the front hall light on, although the house was full of the special silence of sleeping occupants. He quietly mounted the stairs, dropped his clothes on the floor outside the bedroom door, decided to forgo his shower until the morning, and slid quietly into bed. Sally's familiar body warmth enveloped him and he reached over to set the alarm for six-thirty. He was asleep in three minutes.

HE WAS SITTING bolt upright, the bed covers fallen to his waist. It was there before him, almost palpable in the dark bedroom. He was certain of it. He reached forward as though to grasp it, but could not get a grip on it. He squinted into the darkness but couldn't see it. It was there all right, all there. He knew it. The pieces were visible enough but the connective tissue that would pull and shape them into a final structure was not. Occasionally he could sense, almost see, the coalescence between the pieces, but it was always shifting, never clear. At times, there were parts of it that did seem to be clearer, better outlined, but then, teasing and winking and beckoning seductively, it withdrew into formlessness—only to begin to materialize at a different place.

And then, finally, it was completely gone, leaving only floating smoke. Oh, it was there all right, only the more he consciously tried to see through to it, the more obscure it became. He finally gave it up, lay down and pulled the covers up to his chin. In the morning he would try it again.

But in the morning he wasn't even sure if he had been awake or whether it had all been a dream.

# NINETEEN

CONSTANZA DECIDED to see the University people himself and doled out the other names on Stallings's calendar to the others. What they were looking for, he told them, were occasions at which Stallings might have learned about information which could relate to Robertson's murder by, for example, either timing or placement, and thereby make him dangerous enough to kill. He knew it was not something that could be clearly spelled out, and was a long shot, but it had to be covered. He realized a lot of it would depend on their own judgement, and that was why he had asked for them. They agreed to meet back in his office at one o'clock.

After they left, Constanza packed his shoulderbag, smiled softly at the chicken and tomato sandwich Sally had handed him as he had kissed her goodbye that morning, and left the Municipal Building. It was another glorious June morning, the temperature just right for the sweater he had chosen. In spite of the nature of the business he was about, a sense of well-being was impossible to avoid; but, he told himself as he started out, at least he needn't glory in it.

His first stop was Thorndyke's office in the library. Last Saturday, according to the appointments sheet, Stallings had had lunch with Thorndyke at the Thassalos restaurant where, Thorndyke told him, they had discussed the possibility of borrowing some early Elizabethan manuscripts from the Yale library for a new project of his. Stallings wanted to save himself the trip up there. Thorndyke had said he would try, but given the manuscripts' likely condition, doubted that Yale would let them travel, even for so well-known a scholar as Stallings. Constanza checked off Thorndyke.

For Sunday there were two entries on Stallings's calendar, one that read 'Guggenheim Museum', and another that read 'Museum Modern Art—Alex. Nevsky'. Sunday had apparently been recreational culture in New York, at least in the daytime. But Monday looked promising; it had Stallings at the Art Department almost all morning seeing Beecham and Smith-Kohlmer. Constanza checked his bag again and cycled over.

The same secretary who had had nothing but frowns for him three days ago, still had frowns. Christ, was the ability to frown well a prerequisite for the job of departmental secretary? As a matter of fact, he thought, a good frown might be really useful in dealing with intimidatable undergraduates or unwelcome visitors. (One of Sally's complaints about him had always been that he had a very ineffectual frown for raising children.)

The secretary told him almost scoldingly that

Professor Beecham was giving a two-hour class on dating techniques for old canvases, but then admitted grudgingly that Professor Smith-Kohlmer was indeed free and in his office. Constanza toyed with the idea of publicly hauling Beecham out of his class for questioning but finally decided that the idea probably stemmed from his own subconscious desires for grandstanding and his dislike of Beecham's secretary. Instead, he asked the woman to please phone Smith-Kohlmer and tell him he was on his way to see him.

His office was on the first floor next to Lupescu's. Smith-Kohlmer was waiting for him in the doorway and invited him in, but on the way up Constanza had thought of something he had wanted to check with Thorndyke but forgotten and asked if he could please use the phone. Smith-Kohlmer said, sure, and besides he wanted to check something in Lupescu's office, anyway.

Constanza dialled Thorndyke's office. 'Professor Thorndyke, this is Sergeant Constanza. Do you have a minute, please.'

'Sure, Sergeant,' he said. 'What can I do for you that I couldn't do a half-hour ago?'

'Well, I'm afraid I simply forgot to ask you something. In our talk yesterday you were able to place Professor Stallings in the library last Sunday night because someone on your Sunday staff was able to recognize him. I'd like to know how many others could be identified by your people as also having been there Sunday night? I realize that it may have to rely a good deal on memory and the list may not be short. But it may be important. Could you please ask them, sir?'

'Yes, of course I can. And will. And we can do a little better than just relying on memory. We can go over the book check-outs, book requests made that day, things like that. Of course, it will only cover the time up to eight o'clock when the staff leaves for the day. But we'll see what we can come up with. It may take a little time, though. Call me back or drop by my office at, say, around lunchtime. Would that be all right?'

'That'll be just fine, Professor. Thank you very much.'

Constanza hung up and went to get Smith-Kohlmer.

Smith-Kohlmer's office was about a third the size of Beecham's, but since it was one floor higher it had a better view of the campus. Constanza was offered a chair at a small worktable in the middle of the room from which he could look directly out of one of the windows. Smith-Kohlmer sat across from him. Constanza set up his tape recorder and after the initial courtesies and non-committal responses to inquiries about the investigation he started right in. 'Sir, Professor Stallings spent most of last Monday morning talking with you and Professor Beecham. Could you please tell me what about?'

Smith-Kohlmer nodded vigorously. 'So that's what this is all about. Should have guessed, shouldn't I? Poor old Stallings. Terribly gifted man. And such energy. Christ, we should all be that active at that age. Even you, Sergeant.' He put his elbows on the table between them. 'You know what we talked about for over an hour? A new project he was thinking about. Seventy-seven and thinking about his new project after he finishes his current one. Christ.' He shook his head.

'Could you tell me about that, please.'

'Sure. It's an astonishing idea, Sergeant.' He leaned back in his chair and placed his hands behind his neck. 'Stallings is—was—an Elizabethan scholar, among other things. World famous. Now, as you know, in Art there was no Renaissance to speak of in England. Indeed, the nature of whatever Renaissance occurred in England by and large derived from and did not contribute to that remarkable period of breakout and ferment in Italy, France and Germany—the exception, of course, being Elizabethan drama and literature. While Italy, and to a lesser degree the rest of the continent, was painting and sculpting the glories of Florence and Venice and Rome, England was covering canvas with the vacant fish-eyed faces of royalty and inherited privilege. The chief reasons for this were England's insularity, both geographical and temperamental, and the English Reformation which, courtesy of Henry the Eighth, suppressed the expressive arts patroned elsewhere by the Catholic Church and powerful families with good taste. England, instead, developed portraiture and the landscape. These were, of course, safer and more conducive to the maintenance of royal power than the emotions stirred up by what Botticelli and Michelangelo and Titian and Caravaggio were doing. You could get into some very serious trouble depicting the glories of God in the days of Henry and good-looking naked women looking you in the eye in the days of Oliver Cromwell, or even for that matter a hundred years earlier. Granted, England had its share of good artists, but there's really only so much you can do with a face and a pleasant stream, although the genius of Hogarth, Gainsborough and Constable showed you could in fact do quite a lot. Now, what Stallings had in mind was to speculate what might have happened to English Art—hell, English History—if the Renaissance painters of Italy were let loose in England. What would the messages in some of the Renaissance masterpieces have said to England, and the shapers of England, at that time? What would have the Platonic philosophies and the Aristotelian traditions have said to England if they had been translated into English the way Cosimo and Lorenzo de Medici had them translated into Latin? I mean, much of England as we know it today was being formed in those days. What Stallings wanted to do was nothing less than examine a putative Renaissance in England of the type that took place in Italy. Never mind, for the moment, the whole question of the project's validity. Just think of the speculations of a team, or even a pair, of rigorous scholars let loose on a topic like that. Fascinating, eh? What a project. And at the age of seventy-seven!'

In spite of himself Constanza was sufficiently caught up by the idea and Smith-Kohlmer's enthusiasm to remark, 'But as I remember, one of the crucial elements in the Italian Renaissance was a wealthy, powerful and independent merchant class that could supply alternative patronage to either royalty or the Church, something totally missing in England at that time.'

Smith-Kohlmer literally beamed. 'Very good, Sergeant. Quite right. But bear in mind that England *did* have a powerful and, in its own way, independent aristocracy, right?'

'Yes, right,' said Constanza, 'but on the other hand not of a mind to patron the type of art produced by the artists you mentioned.'

He suddenly brought himself up short. Christ, what was going on, here? What the hell were they doing? He was supposed to be investigating a murder.

'Uh, look, Professor, excuse me, but getting back to the present, just what specifically did Stallings want with you?'

'Right. Sorry. Well, what Stallings wanted with me—and/or Beecham—was to discuss collaboration with an art historian. He knew Lupescu, you see—saw him Sunday, he said—and was afraid of his personality in such a venture. And he was right to be afraid. But he thought either Beecham or I might do and might be interested. Beecham was pretty much tied up with administrative work, so that left me. And that's what we talked about for almost two hours on Monday morning. Had a great time and, in fact, made arrangements to talk some more, maybe to begin actually drawing up some plans and approaches. Stallings could be a great intellectual stimulant.' He looked out of the window for a few seconds, then shook his head again. 'What a goddamned shame,' he said softly. He looked up. 'And no, Sergeant, I cannot for the life of me think of any connection between this and his murder.'

But Constanza could. 'Tell me, Professor, Stallings mentioned Caravaggio by name, right?'

'Yes, he did. But a couple of others as well.'

'Did anyone else know of his interest in him, or of this new project he had in mind? I mean, besides you and Beecham.'

'No, not that I know of. That doesn't mean that he didn't talk to others, Sergeant, only that I don't know whom else he might have spoken to about this.'

Smith-Kohlmer suddenly held up a hand. 'Hang on a bit, Sergeant. That's not exactly true.' He was frowning intensely, as though trying to recall something. 'No,' he went on, 'not true at all. During the course of our talk I specifically mentioned Hilda Robertson's thesis. I'm sure I did. And I remember telling him that she might be a good bet. I clearly remember now saying something like there's nothing better than writing a doctoral thesis to get you thoroughly immersed in researching a subject, and that Miss Robertson's subject was very close to what Stallings might want. Christ,' he said, clearly agitated, 'you don't suppose there was any connection between this and her death, do you?'

'I really don't know, Professor. I'm just trying to acquire some facts right now. Do you happen to know if they had known each other?'

'Well, I really don't know,' said Smith-Kohlmer, 'but I don't think so. It was the way he talked about her. You know, what sort of girl was she, was she cooperative, willing to take on projects like this, things like that. I said I just didn't know and we dropped it. Couldn't have spent more than a minute talking about her and then we returned to Stallings's proposals.'

'Would it have been a plum of sorts for someone to have been associated with such a project, teamed up with Stallings?'

'Oh yes. Yes, indeed. Especially for someone like Miss Robertson, just starting out as it were.'

Constanza nodded, then said, 'Changing the subject a bit, do you happen to know if Stallings saw Beecham at all on this?'

'No, he didn't, at least I don't think he did. As I said, we talked almost until lunch-time. I remember him putting on his scarf—he almost always wore one even in the summer months—and saying he would try to catch Beecham some other time.

Except that I know that Beecham was at Pennsylvania University on Wednesday, and Wednesday night poor Stallings was killed. Don't know about Tuesday, though.'

No, but I do, said Constanza to himself, remembering the blank Tuesday on Stallings's calendar.

He nodded again, but this time remained silent. So did Smith-Kohlmer. Constanza could think of nothing further to ask. He sighed, asked if there were anything else Smith-Kohlmer could tell him and, when told no, gathered his belongings and rose to leave. Smith-Kohlmer walked him to the door and, as he shook hands and said goodbye, he added, 'I actually knew Stallings better than the Robertson girl. He was a really brilliant man, and his death is a significant loss. Find the killer, Sergeant. Please find him.'

Constanza was preoccupied as he walked down the stairs and left the building. In fact, he actually forgot that he had wanted to see Beecham, but then decided that it was no great loss.

The problem was how to treat Smith-Kohlmer's information. On the one hand, it might be completely irrelevant; on the other, it might be highly significant, except that if it were he didn't have an inkling of how to tie it into their killing or even into the information he already had.

He strolled to his bicycle, but instead of mounting up and cycling over to the English Department where the other people on Stallings's calendar were located, he put his bag on the ground and leaned against a tree. Was he beginning to amass too much input, too many facts? Was he running a risk here, a danger of sheer quantity of data diluting or even blotting out entirely the truly salient information? Was there a point of diminishing return to consider here? You could probably begin an investigation into anyone's activities, he thought, and begin to accumulate specific facts that after a while could point to...what? An affair with your secretary, a plan to rob a restaurant, a plot to fix a basketball match? You could, by way of selectivity and supposition, build a large assemblage of facts into almost any structure you wanted to—especially when it involved man's behaviour. Well, Friday afternoon was coming up; maybe a good time to sit down in his office for a couple of hours, take some stock and see if some sense could be made of what he already had.

The hour and a half spent at the English Department, all with people he had never met before, brought him no relevant information, for which Constanza was almost grateful. Afterwards, he cycled quickly over to the library to see Thorndyke. He wasn't there, but his secretary had a sealed envelope for him with his name on it. He put it in his bag, checked the time and started back to his office. A little past twelve. His meeting with Howard, Frederick and Cannetti was at one. Fine.

On the way back he stopped off at Frannie's for a bowl of broccoli-bacon soup to eat with his sandwich. Frannie made one homemade soup a day and

Friday's was invariably broccoli-bacon. It was justly famous and she always ran out but Frannie refused to make more than she was comfortable with. But it was only twelve-twenty and there was still plenty.

Mary Underwood was eating yogurt and a bagel at her desk as he called out 'Hi' to her and went immediately to his office. He quickly tore open Thorndyke's envelope. Most of the names were unfamiliar. But Beecham's was there as having checked out two books. Stallings was listed as well, but Constanza already knew that. There were only a dozen others, none whose name figured in the case as far as he knew, but Thorndyke had scribbled on the bottom of the list that he, too, had been at the library in his office from two until about five. Well, nothing much here, he thought. At least nothing that jumped out at him.

Practically one o'clock, now. And, right on cue, first Howard and then almost immediately afterwards Cannetti and Frederick shuffled into his office.

None of them looked enthusiastic or even cheerful. The people they had spoken with had ranged from real estate agents (Stallings was thinking of selling his house and moving into a condominium apartment) to the manager of the local supermarket (Stallings had complained about a bad melon). None of them had any connection with the library, or even with people who had connections with the library. They all seemed to be involved with that

part of Stallings's life unrelated to his work or the
University in general, and could offer nothing even
remotely helpful to the investigation. Well, Constanza told them, it had to be covered. He walked
the officers out, thanked them and said that if anybody ever had any ideas or suggestions, they
should feel free to see either him or Chief Dawson.
On his way back to his office he stopped by at
Mary Underwood's stationery cabinet, got a new
yellow legal pad, and told her he didn't want to be
disturbed for a while.

He sat down at his desk, pulled the pad towards
him and wrote at the head of the top sheet the
question that he still felt was the fulcrum of this
case's solution and his best starting-point: 'What
came to light between Tuesday morning and
Wednesday night that would make Hilda Robertson's killer so fearful that he would kill again to
keep it suppressed?' Then he spread out his written
notes and started playing back his tape-recorder.

For an hour he sat, writing down questions, list-
ing facts and occasionally jotting down what he
thought were promising answers. He quickly covered two pages. At first he crossed out nothing, but
then, as he began to cross-check everything criti-
cally, almost all his answers disappeared as they
led either to nothing constructive or to outright in-
consistencies. But the individual chunks of information, the separate facts that were before him,
inexorably grew.

Soon, a pattern in his theorizing emerged. Two

pieces could be made to fit and form a beginning. Occasionally, a third piece could be successfully added. But anything more would invariably make the chain logically untenable. It was like trying to find a solution as though it were a geometrical exercise; except that nothing, he mocked himself, seemed to be taking shape.

A second hour went by. Constanza was oblivious of the passage of time. Several sheets of paper were by now crumpled up on the floor. He discovered that there was an almost limitless number of possibilities when considering combinations of motive, timing, knowledge and the plausible behaviour of the people involved. At first he had felt that the increasing number of questions was helpful because they were delineating the problem more clearly, but after a while he began to wonder, not for the first time, if all this information might not be counter-productive. From time to time he would look up and gaze blankly around at his surroundings, walls, cabinets, ceiling, wall-clock, trees outside his windows, all without seeing them. He loosened his belt without realizing it. He kicked off his left shoe without noticing.

After the second hour Constanza got up, stretched, made a cup of tea and returned to his desk. He had managed to cover four pages with his scribblings. He took a deep breath, exhaled noisily, and started to go through them again. Midway through the fourth page, two of the pieces he had tried before as a starting-point, but which had led to nothing, were fitted to two others which had been newly written down, and not only were they consistent, they seemed actually to reinforce each other. For the first time, a group as a whole strengthened all the individual parts. Constanza forced himself to go very slowly, not to rush things. But then another piece fell into conformation with the four. And then another. He forgot about his tea. For a long while, a gap stubbornly refused to be filled. Now he did push and try to force pieces, any piece, but nothing worked. A vital link refused to be run down.

He went to the window and opened it, breathing deeply and absorbing the noises of the outside, trying to clear his head. He noticed that one shoe was off and put it back on. He closed the window, returned to the papers on his desk, looked down at the sheet before him and almost immediately jumped up. 'Shit,' he said under his breath. 'Shit,' he said again, more loudly, as though the word itself could invoke success, could make it come out right. The word didn't do it, but Constanza thought of something that might.

He ran to the Mayor's anteroom where the magazines and newspapers were kept, thumbed feverishly through the issue he wanted—and found exactly what he was looking for, what he was certain in his heart he would find. Son of a bitch, it was there. And, just as he had thought, had felt all along, the leap from Stallings's murder to that of

Hilda Robertson became so clear, so facile as to be almost automatic in its appearance.

He ran back to his office and sat, breathing heavily, heart pounding in his ears, with the newspapers, notes, facts, snatches of tape-recordings all before him. He remained frozen, immobile, as the cogs, gears, levers, wheels all fell into place, piece by every piece, until at the end all the parts, all linked and joined, formed the completed structure with no end loose, no gap, every fact perfectly joined to every other.

For a few minutes he just sat, in a state of high excitement, feeling it out, getting accustomed to it. And then he spent an entire hour trying to break it down.

He dredged up time sequences, bits of knowledge, different points of entry into his closed structure, all designed to prove it wrong. But there were so many pieces of so many different shapes all dovetailing so perfectly that all his hammerings at it only seemed to lock it more firmly into place. It had, finally, all the incorruptible strength of geometrical correctness.

# TWENTY

CONSTANZA FORCED himself to breathe normally and walk slowly to Dawson's office. But he almost forgot to knock. Dawson's rule was that he would speak with anyone on the force any time the door was open, but while he never locked his door, if it was closed, you had to knock first.

Dawson yelled, 'Come in,' and Constanza entered, closed the door behind him and sat down in his usual chair facing the lioness. He was trying hard to appear normal but little things were giving him away. His feet were wrapped around the chair legs, his right knee was bouncing up and down and his teeth chewed nervously at the inside of his lip. He clutched his papers a little more tightly and waited quietly until Dawson looked up. Dawson was writing intently, and for a few seconds continued writing as though to finish a sentence before accepting the interruption.

Finally, he pushed himself back from his desk and said, 'Sorry, Phil. I'm just working up a letter to the Chief of Homicide, Philadelphia. I know him. Sanderson. Good guy. It officially requests his aid in a murder investigation here in Kingsford. It cites some shortcomings in facilities and insufficient resources. It explains the delay of the request in terms of very promising early leads producing expectations of rapid developments which, however, did not materialize. It's mostly bullshit and is not going to fool anybody, but the jurisdictions are different and some official piece of paper has to exist. I've written it just in case.' He stopped talking but continued to look at Constanza. 'What's up, Phil?'

Constanza put his papers down on the small conference table and smoothed down one of the corners that had become wrinkled. He tried to sound as matter-of-fact as possible. 'Sam, I want to tell you who killed them, why, and how I know it. And then I want to suggest how I think we can get him. I'll need about thirty minutes.' Constanza was pleased at the steadiness in his voice.

Dawson thrust his head forward and narrowed his eyes. He stayed that way for several seconds, studying Constanza. Finally, he said, 'You're serious, aren't you?' Then he levelled a thick forefinger at Constanza's chest. 'Now you listen to me, Constanza. Just listen to me a minute. We got real troubles on this, troubles all over the fucking map. An hour ago I get a call from Beliveau asking about progress. Fifteen minutes later, surprise, surprise, I get another call from Waterston also asking about progress. And I don't have much to tell them, right? Now you come in here clutching some yellow paper, all piss and vinegar like the fucking cavalry arriving in the nick of time and tell me you've solved these murders. I just want you to know that what I don't need right now is some half-assed, off the wall theorizing full of loose ends and wild assumptions from a guy whom I don't want to hand-hold right now. It's been four days now, right? And that's about the limit for genteel handling and highblown intellectual conjecture. Time is fast approaching to shit or get off the pot. Now, are you sure you want to go ahead with your dramatics?'

Constanza had never heard Dawson's voice like this; it was tense, it filled the room and it contained genuine menace.

'I still want thirty minutes, Sam,' Constanza said as calmly as he could, 'and I also want to use your blackboard.'

Dawson grimaced with displeasure, waited a few seconds until he became placid, then picked up the phone and told Mary Underwood no calls, no visitors. He turned to Constanza. 'Take a whole fucking hour.'

Constanza spread out his papers on the table and began. After ten minutes he started using the blackboard. After fifteen Dawson started asking questions. Soon he was telling Constanza to 'wait a minute, wait a minute' followed by long silences, ending with 'OK, go on.' Constanza finished after forty minutes. It had not gone as smoothly as he would have liked, but it was, after all, a first run-through, and besides, he hadn't counted on Dawson's interruptions. He returned to his chair, arranged his spread-out papers back into a neat pile and looked at Dawson. 'That's it,' he said.

For a while, neither of them spoke. Dawson rose, walked to the window, raised it, put some birdseed on the outside sill, closed the window and returned slowly to his chair. Still nobody spoke. The silence grew into expectancy. Constanza was damned if he was going to be the one to break the silence. He knew he had made sense but had no idea what was going on in Dawson's mind, and Dawson's facial expression wasn't giving any clues. During the presentation his demeanour had indicated only scepticism, although the naked irritation had left his voice. Also, Constanza considered his questions a positive sign, an indication that he wasn't dismissing it out of hand. But acceptance was another matter.

Dawson finally took a deep breath and said, 'And you figured all this out just from your papers there?'

'Just from the facts, Sam. And what people have told us.' He motioned to the neat pile of papers. 'It's all there. I didn't make any of it up.'

'No, you didn't, Phil.' Dawson stretched out his legs, arched his torso, looked up at the ceiling and yawned hugely. 'You make one hell of a case. Damned hard to disagree with. Damned hard. Even the craziness in it has the ring of behaviourial truth.'

Dawson became quiet again, swivelled his chair and looked out of the windows. The late afternoon

sun was slanting sharply into the room at this time
of day and the elongated window patterns on the
floor had reached all the way across and had begun
to glide up the far wall. Heavy suspensions of dust
motes were clearly visible in the sun's rays.

The fact of the matter was that Dawson felt
somewhat at a loss. Here I am, he was thinking to
himself, in the fourth day of our investigation.
Minimal progress. Waterston and that idiot Beliveau making no bones about how they feel about
my calling in outside help. And I'm already partially resigned to doing that. And suddenly, out of
the blue, my detective comes up with a solution to
these murders at once bizarre as hell and, God help
me, almost irrefutable. He had been caught up in
the story, no getting around it. He had even enjoyed its exposition in a detached, disinterested
sense. As an intellectual exercise, he could savour
it. He could even be comfortable with Constanza's
innocent sense of achievement. But take it to
court? Even base an arrest on it?

Except what else did he have, and what was the
alternative?

'Phil, it's good detective work and downright
extraordinary deductive reasoning, assuming it's
true. Christ, it's not bad even if it's *not* true. But
you can't make an arrest on it because you can't
base a trial on it. And you know it, right? Besides,
if I remember, you were going to tell me how
you're going to get him.'

'Yes, but you're going to have to give me five more minutes.'

This time Dawson laughed out loud. 'You're really enjoying yourself, aren't you? Well, I hope it turns out you deserve it. Go ahead. After that story you've put together I'm willing to listen to almost anything you lay on me.'

Ten minutes later Dawson was nodding his head and saying, 'You know what I like about all this? The worst that can happen to us is embarrassment and disappointment. And I was all set for that, anyhow.' He reached for the phone.

'Dr Thorndyke? Chief of Police Dawson. I have Sergeant Constanza here in my office and we would like to stop by... Yes, now... Well, we would like to put a proposition to you and, yes, it's quite important... We can be there in ten minutes... Splendid. And thank you very much, sir.'

Next, he called Charlie Harris at the *Chronicle*. 'Charlie? Sam Dawson. Look, Phil Constanza and I want to come over and talk over something with you... Yes, it's about the killings... No, we've got to do it in person... Yes, now, except we've got to make a stop first. How about we see you in half an hour... I know it's Friday afternoon, Charlie, but I'm afraid we've got to see you and it's got to be soon... Fine. It's appreciated. So long, Charlie.'

He made his final call to the Ace Security Services in Trenton. 'Elwood? This is Sam Dawson in Kingsford... Right... I'm just fine, Elwood...

Yes, there is. I need some help from you and I hope you won't disappoint me... The thing of it is, Elwood, I need it tonight and it may take a couple of hours, maybe more. I know it's Friday and if there were any other way I'd do it but there isn't. I'll get you a good price from the municipality, Elwood. What do you say?... Terrific. I knew you would. And I owe you a big one. Now, here's the deal.'

# TWENTY-ONE

WHILE THORNDYKE was immediately agreeable to the plan, Charlie Harris was less than enthusiastic, citing ethical qualms about printing information in his newspaper that he knew was false. Dawson pointed out that in a manner of speaking the information was in fact not false. Harris nodded but was still reluctant, saying Dawson was practising sophistry. Dawson persevered, finally saying that dainty ethical considerations in the circumstances might seem a bit self-indulgent. He didn't smile. Harris got the message, said he would have no trouble breaking into tomorrow's front page as long as they kept it to about two hundred words and got it to the composing room in two hours' time. Dawson said that was no problem and they immediately began working on it. Charlie Harris himself supplied the heading, BOOKS MAY HELP NAB KILLER.

'AH, SO GLAD I caught you. Clement Thorndyke here and please forgive me for calling you at home... Well, in a few minutes you may not think it such a pleasure. I'm calling from Chicago, you see. I'm in a bit of a bind and would like to ask

you to do me a very big favour... Well, it's most
kind of you but let me describe the situation first.
Yesterday we got permission from the police to
clean up the sites on the A and D levels of the
library where those poor people were killed... Yes,
I know. Grisly business... Well, it was affecting
the students, you see, and I was keen to restore
things to normal as quickly as possible. So we ti-
died things up a bit, took down the yellow police
tape and all that, and of course we cleaned up and
reshelved the books that were being used by the
victims when they were killed. Now, last night I
got a call from Police Chief Dawson—Sam Dawson, I believe—saying that he is thinking of calling
in the Philadelphia Police to assist in the investigation... Well, as I understand it they've simply
not been able to make any progress here at all in
the matter... Right... In the event, the point of his
call was that they want to restore all the material
evidence at the scenes of the crime, including the
books. Dawson mumbled something about the
books possibly being more valuable in the investigation than they had initially thought. As a result
I promised to have the books in my office for him
by noon today. Now, what happened was that in
the midst of my preparing for this Chicago trip I
simply forgot all about it. My secretary is away for
two days, the weekend staff are notoriously un-
trustworthy and I've committed myself to getting
those books for Dawson. I know that you sometimes spend Saturday morning in the library—met

you there a couple of times if you recall—and was wondering if perhaps you had plans to be there today and, if so, could you please... Oh, that would be grand... Yes, it's three Caravaggio books that the poor Robertson girl had been working on in her carrel. They're by Larghini, Calvesi and Marini. They were reshelved just yesterday and I'm sure you'll have no trouble locating them. Right up your alley and shelved pretty close together, I would guess... Right. Just so. I've already phoned ahead and told security to leave the door to my office open, so all you have to do is just pop in and leave them on my desk... Marvellous. It's a great load off my mind. I'll be returning Wednesday night and perhaps we can have lunch on Thursday... Excellent. And, again, I can't thank you enough... Right. Goodbye.'

THORNDYKE HAD OFFERED to help but Dawson politely reminded him that he was supposed to be in Chicago. In fact, Dawson had said, it would be a very good idea if both he and his wife stayed indoors all Saturday morning until twelve; he was sure Thorndyke would understand.

Constanza and Dawson arrived at the library at seven-thirty just to ensure that they would have plenty of time before its opening. They went directly to Thorndyke's office, let themselves in and arranged a couple of chairs near the door so that when it swung open anyone entering would have to come well into the room before they would be seen. They made themselves comfortable and settled down to wait. Dawson had actually brought a book to read. 'That's me,' he said, 'bringing a book to read into the library.'

Constanza had not brought a book; it had not even occurred to him. In the end, he had decided to surrender to what he really was, and simply resigned himself to living with his nervousness. He bit his nails and let his mind wander.

At first, he thought about last night. Sally had waited up for him even though he hadn't gotten home until midnight. As usual, she had made a platter for him and not until she had heated it in the microwave and the smell reached him did he realize how hungry he was. He wolfed the food down in large mouthfuls, barely pausing to chew. Sally opened a bottle of beer ('it'll help you sleep') and poured it into a large glass. That went in two large draughts.

After a while, the food and the beer began to do their work, and he began to unwind.

'The kids have been asking about you,' she said. 'I have, too.'

'Well, it's this thing, Sal,' he said. 'So much to do. So much legwork.' He shrugged, then was silent for a while. The lateness of the hour and the two of them huddled over the kitchen table lent a special intimacy to their conversation. Then: 'It's almost like a personal thing, Sal, you know? I mean, it's my job, right? It's what I'm supposed to do, supposed to be able to do. But it's new to me. I mean, we've never done anything like this before. And it's not textbooks or Cliff notes or final exams. It's me. It's what I do here in Kingsford. And Dawson. But mostly me. And the thing of it is I've got nothing to reference to, you know? Nothing to clue me on whether I'm doing it right or not. Christ, sometimes I get the feeling I'm re-inventing the wheel, and I really should be past that, should be better than that.' Sally nodded sympathetically, wanting to ask if there were anything she could do and knowing that there wasn't. 'See, my place here in Kingsford is very publicly defined and I'm going to be seen in this thing not through my bicycle or my sweaters or even by my badge ID, but by what, if anything, I cause to happen when the biggest law on the books gets broken.' For a few seconds he fidgeted quietly, then continued: 'You see, Sal, sometimes we are what we make or what we think, and sometimes we are only our consequences, what we make happen. It's that simple. And that's as it should be.' He stopped again and, as though for emphasis, lightly took hold of her fingers. 'I don't know how this is going to come out, Sal, and it bothers me. This isn't like stopping a car on the Turnpike or testifying in court on a car theft, where the scenarios and the conclusions are pretty much set. We wrote this scenario as we went along, and the conclusion is, well, completely up in the air. See, we've got something going, Sam and I. We're trying something and I can't tell you anything about it, but... You see,

Sal, I made it all up, and maybe it's true and maybe we'll find out tomorrow. And, then again, maybe not.' He sighed. 'But one way or the other, I think after tomorrow it's going to change for us here in Kingsford. Back to normal hours, and that pretty damn soon.'

She had smiled, said that sometimes it was all right to be nervous and that she loved him. She slid her hand inside his pants and kissed him good night and told him to come upstairs whenever he wanted to. It had been one-thirty before he decided to risk trying to sleep.

Now he was seated in Thorndyke's office wondering if Dawson, ten feet away idly reading *Flaubert's Parrot* actually was that calm or if he was just putting it on.

Constanza thought it through all over again. No, still no holes in the reasoning. The hole was in the unknown human response. Even if he was spot-on right, there was still no telling what would happen afterwards, what everybody's reactions would be as things developed. At times like this he envied the certainty possessed by the genuinely religious.

The door knob turned at nine-thirty, and a man entered. For one second Constanza closed his eyes tightly, then opened them; there had been one sledge-hammer heartbeat in his chest and one deep intake of breath, and afterwards a surprising dispassion. He had gone over it in his mind countless times during the last twelve hours and now there remained only the doing of it.

He started in.

'Sir,' he said to the man, 'may I see those books, please?' He took the books, read the authors' names on the spines and held them up to show Dawson, who was now standing, too. 'We were right, Sam. Exactly right.'

Dawson nodded, trying to look and sound businesslike. 'It's your collar, Phil.'

The man had been rigid with surprise since Constanza's first words. Then, as Dawson spoke he had turned towards him. Now he turned back to Constanza, face still full of shock and confusion.

'Professor Stefan Lupescu, you are under arrest, charged with the murders of Hilda Robertson and Alardyce Stallings. You have the right to remain silent. You have the right to a lawyer. If you do not have, or cannot afford, a lawyer, one will be appointed for you free of charge. If you choose not to remain silent, anything you say can and will be used against you in a court of law.'

Lupescu's body remained rigid but his eyes were telling the story. At first frozen with surprise, then unfocused and moving wildly as the mind struggled to focus and comprehend, and finally settling down and narrowing slightly as the intellect caught up and control was reasserted.

'Chief of Police Dawson and Sergeant, ah, Constanza, is it not?' he said. 'We met a couple of days ago, isn't that so? Well, just what is happening here? Can you please tell me what is happening?'

'Yes, sir,' said Constanza. 'You are being arrested for murder.'

Lupescu turned again to look at Dawson, then back to Constanza. 'You *are* serious, aren't you?'

'Yes, sir.'

Lupescu was silent. You could almost see the wheels in his head grinding into motion, almost hear the debate going on as to how to handle this, what attitude to take and what to say. Constanza reckoned that for a man like Lupescu, with his background, the decision on how exactly to respond might be somewhat more complicated because while it was true that he and Dawson represented police authority, it was certainly different from what it might be in Romania. Lupescu might be having trouble simply finding some familiar reference points in dealing with police.

Finally, in a tone of voice which managed to include ill humour, bluster and genuine curiosity, he said, 'But why are you doing this? Do you have a basis for it?'

Constanza and Dawson had discussed this situation the night before, and they had decided that while it would definitely suit their purpose to present Lupescu eventually with everything they had, the manner in which it was doled out could strongly affect the situation. What they were after, the single best thing that could happen, was a free confession after a proper Miranda warning, and overwhelming him with how much they knew was, they thought, the best way to achieve that. But of course, much of that now depended on Lupescu's responses.

Constanza was still holding the books. Lupescu eyed them and suddenly said, 'Do those books have something to do with this?'

'Yes, they do,' said Constanza.

'Well, then you might wish to know,' said Lupescu, 'that Clement Thorndyke, head of the library, asked me to fetch those books and leave them here on his desk.'

'No, that's not quite right,' said Constanza. 'Thorndyke asked for the books found in Hilda Robertson's study carrel after she was murdered, books that he said were written by Larghini, Calvesi and Marini. But you brought books written by Larghini, Calvesi and Bavi.' He held up the books he had taken from Lupescu. 'He asked for the wrong books, Professor Lupescu, but you brought the right ones.'

Lupescu's jaw dropped and he scowled fiercely as he grappled with it. He plopped down into a visitor's chair at the side of Thorndyke's desk and stared at the wall. Dawson walked slowly to where Constanza was standing and they both sat down in chairs facing Lupescu.

Lupescu suddenly swivelled his eyes to Constanza. 'But it was Thorndyke who told me what books to get and who gave me the authors' names. Yes, I remember distinctly.'

'No,' said Constanza, 'he gave you Marini, not Bavi.'

'No, no, Sergeant, I am absolutely sure it was—'

'We have a recording of the phone conversation, Professor.'

Lupescu seemed genuinely perplexed. 'But Thorndyke called me from Chicago this morning.'

'Clement Thorndyke never left Kingsford, Professor. He has been at his home on Regent's Lane all morning. He made that call at our request.'

Lupescu exhaled slowly and said softly, 'And the item in the *Chronicle* this morning...?'

'Was also a plant, Professor, to push you a little to examine the books just in case you thought there was something that you might have overlooked. Again, you chose the right books.'

Lupescu licked his lips. 'Listen,' he said nervously, 'I gave that list to some clerk at the circulation desk this morning. I don't remember what she looked like too well, but she got them for me. She might have gotten the right authors from someone, some friend, I don't know. How can you...?'

'We had a surveillance camera installed in the stacks, Professor. You were video-recorded taking the books yourself.' Constanza, of course, wasn't sure that the recording had been made; after all, some electronic failure might have occurred. But he was so sure about his thinking now, that he was certain Lupescu wouldn't notice it.

Lupescu's hands fell to his side and his head sagged.

Sam Dawson had witnessed this scene played

out many times before in interrogation rooms in Philadelphia, and he knew that, contrary to what most people might think, the best thing to do now was to remain silent. At this stage you let the guy try to get himself out from under, let him think up his own escape attempts—and then knock down every one of them. Kicking the bottom out of a guy's own reasoning had always proved much more psychologically damaging than simply volunteering your information. So far, Constanza was doing just fine. In fact, Dawson was marvelling at his composure. As far as he knew this was a first for him.

Lupescu was raising his head again. 'Sergeant, it really was impossible for me to know the "right" books, as you call them. Look, they were never made public. I believe the *Chronicle* was the only newspaper that even mentioned any books and they gave neither title nor author. And I never even saw the scene of the crime, so how could I possibly know?'

'Because,' said Constanza, 'you had, over the course of time, checked them out of the library using Leonard Friedman's card and dropped them off in the book drop last Sunday night. So that Hilda Robertson would be able to get them, the most important source books for her thesis, and be using them in her study carrel Monday night.'

It was a crucial moment and while Constanza remained apparently placid Dawson anxiously shifted his feet, took his hands from his pockets and folded them in his lap.

And after a few seconds they knew they had him, that everything that Constanza had worked out was right. Because Lupescu did not look up quizzically and say, Leonard Friedman?... Who's that? Or deny being in the library Sunday night. Or even ask if they could prove that. He just sat there, limp as a half-full sack of old clothes, rheumy eyes staring, the very image of someone found out.

But it didn't last very long. Stefan Lupescu, formed by an upbringing in the world of the Balkans, international authority on Renaissance art, flouter of conventions, most prestigious member of the Kingsford Art Department, was not about to roll over without a struggle.

'But you cannot prove any of this nonsense you are saying. How can you...?'

'Alardyce Stallings told Professor Smith-Kohlmer that he had seen you last Sunday in the library. But according to Stallings's appointments calendar he was in New York all day; that, and the fact that the library staff did not register your entrance during normal hours means that Stallings must have seen you in the library in the evening.'

'But this is preposterous, totally.' Lupescu's gaze shifted from Constanza to Dawson, but Dawson was playing Constanza's game, keeping his face impassive and simply staring back at Lupescu. 'I mean, none of this connects me in the slightest way with the actual fact of killing both these people.'

'Yes, it does, Professor. It provides the link. It explains why you had to kill Stallings. You see, the book return records show that those three books were returned sometime during Sunday night after normal working hours. That's why you had to kill Stallings; he saw you returning those three books Sunday night.'

'But this is more nonsense. He had absolutely no knowledge that those books were important to the murders. If—*if* mind you—what you say is true, why should I fear him for that?'

'But you didn't fear him at first, Professor, not until Wednesday, until the *Chronicle* mentioned three books on Caravaggio found at the murder scene. That's why, even though you had the same opportunity on Tuesday, you didn't kill him until Wednesday. That's when you realized he could implicate you, that he could cause it all to unravel. And as long as he lived there would always be that possibility, the possibility that one day, one night, on a train, in a restaurant, the thought would occur to him that Stefan Lupescu had returned three Caravaggio books to the library the day before those same books were found at the scene of a murder. By itself, maybe nothing. But just one idle thought, just one or two questions to start things in motion, and it would be enough.'

Constanza's geometry was beginning to sink in on Lupescu. He paused, and again Constanza and

Dawson could see his mind working over all the pieces, how each one fitted, how they connected and then drew the next piece in. And again they remained silent.

'But if he knew that on Wednesday morning,' said Lupescu, 'why didn't he call you, or someone, and report that. Surely Professor Stallings would realize the significance of that.'

'Because,' said Constanza, 'Professor Stallings had not read that morning's issue of the *Chronicle*. When I visited his house on Thursday I found Wednesday's issue still folded up in his driveway.'

Lupescu began taking very deep breaths, one right after the other, as though his body had been methodically deprived of oxygen at a very slow rate until it realized suddenly that it was starving for it.

He sat again with his head bowed. This time he didn't even bother raising his eyes, but spoke dully, almost fearfully. 'I had absolutely no reason to kill that girl, no reason at all.'

This time Constanza spoke softly. 'That's not true, sir. You did have—for you, for what you are, for where you are coming from.' The words had come to Constanza almost reflexively, as the key that had unlocked it all. 'You had a very strong reason. Jealousy.'

'Oh, please,' said Lupescu, 'don't be ridiculous. Jealous of that mediocre neophyte, of that unpublished upstart who had to sleep with the Department head to get a promotion, of that—?'

'No, Professor. Jealous of the rival who was stealing your lover from you.'

The crumbling occurred slowly and in stages. First, the eyes glazed and became lifeless, then the mouth sagged loosely and a small gob of spittle ran down the chin. The shoulders slumped forward and the long skinny arms dropped almost to the floor. For a moment Constanza thought Lupescu might actually fall, but then he propped himself up by placing his elbows on his knees. For a while he just sat like that, hands limp, a now noticeable tremor in his left arm. Then he slowly brought his hands up and buried his face in them.

Again there was silence, the only sound being Lupescu's sibilant breathing. Constanza's impassivity was beginning to seem eerie and Dawson couldn't read him any more. This time Dawson broke in. Constanza had been brilliant but he couldn't chance losing the moment. He leaned forward. 'Professor Lupescu,' he said quietly, 'I really believe that it would be easier on you if you were to make a statement, tell us all about it, get it off your chest and unburden your mind. You'll feel much the better for it. It's really all over, you know. One way or the other, it's really all over. We do have all the pieces. The only concern now is how it all happens after we leave here.'

Lupescu dropped his hands and seemed to be thinking. Then, without any other part of him moving, Lupescu raised his eyelids and looked balefully at Dawson. After a while he said, 'Does Beecham have to be mentioned?'

It was a request, almost a supplication, delivered in little more than a whisper. It surprised both of them, but it was Dawson, very quick off the mark, who immediately saw it as an unexpected lever of persuasion. He didn't hesitate. 'I believe not, Professor,' he continued quietly, 'I believe we can have language in the statement that would circumvent that.'

'And Beecham will be informed that his name will not be mentioned in this matter?' said Lupescu.

'I will see to it personally, Professor,' said Dawson.

Both their heads moved slightly and something tangible seemed to flow from Dawson to Lupescu. Constanza, wary of disturbing things even in the slightest, sat as though transfixed.

There was another long pause.

'And you really think I'll feel better afterwards?' said Lupescu plaintively.

'I've seen it a dozen times, Professor,' said Dawson, still quietly but with more firmness now.

In the silence the ticking of the wall clock was like hammer blows on cast iron.

Lupescu nodded, more to himself than to anyone else in the room. 'You'll want to take this down, I suppose.'

Almost in unison Constanza and Dawson pulled themselves upright in their chairs and exhaled.

'Yes, sir,' said Constanza as he pulled the tape-recorder from his bag and clicked it on.

A half-hour later Sam Dawson went to get Mary Underwood from the main reading-room where she had been waiting, gave her the recorder and a set of miniature earphones, and led her to a partitioned bank of wordprocessors and printers. An hour later Lupescu's statement had been transcribed to a floppy disk, three copies printed out, and all sheets signed by Lupescu and witnessed by Mary Underwood and Philip Constanza. Mary Underwood was next told to make two back-up disks and six photocopies of the confession and lock everything, including the original audio cassette tape from Constanza's recorder, in the police department safe. She was to be accompanied by Officer Frederick, in uniform, whose job it would be to protect the records from becoming public in case of any trouble on the way over. Stefan Lupescu was then unobtrusively escorted out of the library by Officers Kennedy and Cannetti, not in uniform, who had also been waiting in the main reading-room, and taken to a cell in the basement of the Municipal Building where he was given the names of half a dozen criminal lawyers and told he could make as many phone calls as he wished so long as they were either to lawyers or relatives.

It was not until after Lupescu had been removed from Thorndyke's office that Dawson and Constanza dismantled the recording camera that had been video-taping the entire interrogation. 'You never can tell about trials, Phil. Amazing how people's recollections about coerced confessions can be activated when prodded by an energetic defence lawyer.'

They looked around, checked the office for a last time and made sure they locked the door when they left. They took the Caravaggio books with them.

THEY WERE VERY QUIET during lunch, sandwiches again at Frannie's. Dawson tried repeatedly to open Constanza up but was not successful. Actually, Constanza had been quiet ever since Lupescu had started giving his statement; it had been Dawson who had handled all the mechanical and legal details during Lupescu's confession, and steered him to ways around mentioning Beecham. The motivating forces for Hilda Robertson's murder had become professional jealousy, severe paranoia, and a character moulded by the violence of Eastern Europe.

Constanza was eating a grilled cheese sandwich very deliberately, eyes fixed on the middle distance. Half way through he stopped and said that he was getting stomach cramps. He had turned a little pale and a light sheen of perspiration had appeared on his forehead.

'Christ, I don't know what it is with me, Sam, but I can't seem to untie my stomach. It should be over by now, shouldn't it?'

'Listen, Phil, can I give you some advice?' said Dawson.

'Sure.'

Dawson reached into his pocket and brought out a roll of antacid tablets. 'Take three or four of these. Drink some water. Call Sally, tell her it's all over and that everything's fine, but there are some things, papers, you've got to take care of and you'll be home in a few hours. Then ride your bike over to Mallison gym, do an hour on the nautilus machine and twenty or thirty laps in the pool. Go home, take a very hot shower, have a couple of drinks before dinner. Watch some idiot TV or a baseball game. You'll probably get sleepy sooner than you think. If you want to get laid and can't get it up, don't worry. Sally's a smart girl and will understand more than you think. You should be fine in the morning.'

Constanza thought a bit, then nodded and said, 'Sounds good.' He suddenly looked hard at Dawson. 'And just how, by the way, do you come by all this medical wisdom?'

Dawson made a face. 'You're such a damned hotshot detective, why don't you try and figure it out?'

Constanza smiled for the first time that day, and as he took the roll of tablets from Dawson he said, 'What are you going to do this afternoon?'

'Get on the phone and arrange a meeting for tomorrow afternoon. You're going to be there, too, and I'll fill you in about seven o'clock this evening when I've got all the details.'

# TWENTY-TWO

THE FOUR OF THEM were seated around Sam Dawson's conference table occupying the same chairs they had five days ago. Everyone was aware of it, yet by some tacit agreement no one mentioned it. There was a copy of Lupescu's confession before each of them, although only George Beliveau and Gerald Waterston were reading theirs. Dawson, Constanza and Beliveau wore open-necked shirts, very much in line with a bright Sunday afternoon in June. Dawson and Beliveau were in summer slacks, Constanza in chinos. Waterston had on a three-piece worsted suit whose sole acknowledgement of the season and temperature was its light weight. Dawson had opened both windows, admitting a light breeze along with the occasional rustling and chirping noises of spring. The customary human sounds of midweek on campus were notably absent.

The meeting had been arranged by Dawson. Waterston had agreed immediately. Beliveau had at first begged off, but when Dawson had told him that it was going to be the only time he had planned to have the four of them together to discuss the case in its entirety ('And if you can't make it, George, I'll have Mary type up a short memo for you tomorrow.') he quickly assented.

Constanza and Dawson were, of course, familiar with the statement and gazed idly out of the windows while Waterston and Beliveau read. Waterston was slowly and continually running his fingers through his hair. He was clearly disturbed and uncomfortable, frowning and pursing his lips and shifting in his chair as he read of how one of his academic luminaries had plotted, schemed and ultimately committed heinous murder in his University. Beliveau sat motionless but his responses were more visceral, occasionally murmuring 'damn' or 'shit', sometimes rereading phrases and actually moving his lips around the complexities of Lupescu's speech. Two or three times he stopped reading altogether, gazed at Constanza or Dawson for a few seconds as though to comment, and then returned, close-mouthed, to his reading. They finally finished, exhaled almost in unison and looked up.

Dawson started right in and didn't mince words. 'I've brought you here mainly for two reasons. The first is that we, Constanza and I, consider that some of what we have here—' he held up his copy of the confession—'reflects on the University, and while this is now public domain, and should be, some of what ripples out from this is not and need not be. For example, Hilda Robertson had a student boyfriend who is not mentioned here. No need for it, and it would only cause distress. It may get out eventually but will not be in any official police document. The point is that we have no intention of disclosing at this time anything more than what is in these pages. To spell it out a bit further, the Police Department's approach in dealing with the public in general and the press in particular will include damage control to the University. The town itself really doesn't need anything like that. We will stick to facts, decry rumours and insinuations, and discourage speculation. If need be, we will hide behind the legal barrier of not discussing details before a possible upcoming trial, as we in fact should. We are treating this whole matter as the unfortunate aberration of one single individual. You people are free to say whatever you wish to reporters, faculty, students, electorate, whatever, but keep in mind the context.' Dawson then spoke more slowly for emphasis. 'I don't think it would be a good idea for the University President, the Mayor of Kingsford and the town police to be seen going off in different directions here. The Department, which means mainly me, will issue a final press release to whoever wants to see it that will carry the confession's major points.' He paused. 'Is anybody uncomfortable with any of this?'

Waterston nodded. Beliveau looked up at Dawson and smiled blandly. 'Who are you protecting, Sam?'

Dawson looked him squarely in the face and said, 'The University, the town, and some people to whom we've promised confidentiality, George, if possible. Any objections?'

'Oh, not from me,' said Beliveau hastily, 'not from me.'

'Glad to hear it, George,' said Dawson.

There was silence for a few seconds. 'And the second reason we're here,' said Dawson, 'is that I want you to hear how this case was solved, that is, how Constanza here solved it, so that we'll all have a common information base. It was a brilliant piece of work by one smart, hard-working guy and he deserves both the credit and the embarrassment he's going to get for it. He's going to go over with you how its completeness, and the incontestability of its logic, were chiefly responsible for breaking down Lupescu and producing his confession. Please feel free to ask any questions you want.' And, he said to himself, we'll see how he handles the first public critique of his story, now sanitized by the omission of Lupescu's and Beecham's relationship. 'Starting tomorrow,' he went on, 'I'm going to refer all questions to the investigating officer, namely Constanza here. Phil, why don't you go ahead, now?'

For a second time Constanza went through the events, the facts and the reasoning that led him to Lupescu. The logic was not quite so strong as it had been when he had first presented it to Dawson because he substituted Lupescu's professional jealousy and a paranoid's violence for the jealousy of a homosexual lover. On the other hand, the success of the Caravaggio books gambit now dominated the story and effectively overshadowed everything else. In the end there was unstinting praise, admiration and gratitude from Waterston, but something less from Beliveau whose response was somehow reserved and vaguely grudging. Beliveau, in fact, was giving the impression of being in some way let down. Dawson, not caught up in Constanza's account, was the only one who noticed it. Finally, when Beliveau remarked that things seemed to have gotten resolved neatly and tidily with a minimum of fuss, Dawson understood. Beliveau was disappointed that the University hadn't been sullied any more than by being merely the setting for some ordinary run-of-the-mill jealousy. He would have preferred a little more dirty linen so he could snicker at the University and its inherent power over the town.

After the questions died down Beliveau looked around the table and said, 'You know, I remember only a few days back that we didn't really know what to do here or even how to do it. And, of course, we were just yesterday thinking of calling in Philadelphia.' He held up the confession. 'You guys have really lucked out on this.' He swivelled quickly to Constanza, 'Uh, no offence, Sergeant. Terrific work you've done here.'

'Well, George,' said Dawson, 'better to be lucky than smart, I always say. Now, if there's nothing else, I'm sure there are other things we either want, or have, to do on an afternoon like this.'

As Waterston and Beliveau rose to leave, Dawson said, 'Professor Waterston, would you stay, please. There are just a couple of minor technical things I'd like to go over with you.'

Beliveau looked back at Dawson's impassive face, hesitated a moment, then said goodbye and left.

Dawson rose, locked the door, then turned to Waterston. 'You run the University, Waterston, and as far as I can tell, you do it well. Everyone I talk to says so. Also I hear you're a good guy. So in the interests of your having as much knowledge as possible to enable you to continue to do your best possible job I want you to see a part of the video-recording we made of Lupescu's actual interrogation. No one knows about it except us three, and we're going to keep it that way. No exceptions. No vitiating circumstances. Are you agreed?'

Waterston, perplexed, nodded. Dawson shook his head. 'I don't want a confused nod here, Waterston. I want a clear and firm yes.'

This time Waterston looked directly at him and said, 'Yes, I understand. Yes, I agree. No reservations, no hedging. Now, what is this all about?'

'Fine,' said Dawson, 'I'll show you.' He went to the television set in the corner, slid a video-cassette cartridge into its loading slot and turned the set on. Operating the search controls, he quickly found the section in which the real motive for Hilda Robertson's murder was discussed. They watched and listened in silence. After it was finished, Dawson turned the set off and withdrew the cartridge from its carriage. Waterston looked down at the confession still before him. His face had become ashen. For a long time he was motionless, an expression of enormous sadness on his face. Dawson and Constanza were also quiet, giving Waterston as much time as he needed to absorb fully what they had shown him. Finally, with an effort, he raised his shoulders and whispered, 'God. Good God almighty.'

'Only the three of us, Waterston,' said Dawson. 'Can you do that?'

Waterston cleared his throat, then again whispered, 'Yes, I can do that. I'm really not as weak as I look.'

'I know that, sir,' said Dawson. 'Otherwise I wouldn't have shown you that.'

'And,' said Waterston in a much stronger voice, 'I presume you know how much I...the University...are in your debt. And also that this...this... good thing you have done will never be publicly acknowledged.'

'That's the whole point, sir,' said Dawson.

With some effort, Waterston slowly pulled himself up, then fully straightened himself and formally shook hands with both Dawson and Constanza. 'Fine and good work, gentlemen. Truly. It has been a literal pleasure to know you.'

After he left, Dawson turned to Constanza and said, 'You should be feeling pretty damn good right now, Phil. We both should.'

Constanza nodded. 'What do I do now, Sam?'

'All you do now is be bothered by people for a few days. Then testify at a trial if there is one. And that's all.'

Constanza nodded. 'And what about you, Sam? What are you going to do?'

Dawson didn't answer. Instead he said, 'You know, I got real pissed at Beliveau. I swear the guy seemed actually put out that we pulled this off by ourselves and that the University isn't going to get quite the black eye it could have gotten. What am I going to do? I think I'm going to run for mayor in November and whip his ass, that's what.'

Constanza was stunned, then smiled. 'What?' he said. 'You're joking, right?'

'I joke you not, Phil.'

Constanza's smile broadened. 'A Republican? Sam Dawson a Republican? What are—'

'Hold it, Phil. Hold it. As a Democrat. And I'm really serious about this. Tell me, what do you think?'

'Sam, now you *are* joking. This town hasn't had a Democratic mayor in almost half a century. And a Black?' Constanza shook his head.

'Right,' said Dawson, 'and I think the double-barrelled novelty of it all, plus riding the coat-tails of this case for all it's worth after your story comes out next week, might just be enough to get me in.'

He suddenly smacked his hands together. 'Shit, I got speeches to write and IOUs to call in.' He headed for the door, then paused with his hands on the knob. 'Hell, I've even got the perfect replacement when I vacate my current office.'

# FAMILY PRACTICE
## Charlene WEIR

### A Susan Wren Mystery

**"Susan Wren…is a winner."**
**—*Mostly Murder***

The Barringtons are a wealthy family—prominent
and respected in their small town. All but the youngest
are doctors. Then the eldest, Dorothy, is shot to death—
gunned down—in her office. But there is a surviving
witness to this heinous crime: eleven-year-old
Jen Bryant has also been shot, but not mortally wounded.

As the young girl struggles for each breath in hospital,
police chief Susan Wren begins an investigation that
opens up a Pandora's box of dark, tormented secrets in
the prominent Barrington family. As two more lives are
claimed, the former big-city cop must follow a grisly trail
to a truth as tragic as the crimes.

**"A slam-bang finish."** **—*Kirkus Reviews***

Available in May 1997 at your favorite retail stores.

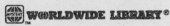

# Take 3 books and a surprise gift FREE

## SPECIAL LIMITED-TIME OFFER

**Mail to:** The Mystery Library™
3010 Walden Ave.
P.O. Box 1867
Buffalo, N.Y. 14240-1867

**YES!** Please send me 3 free books from the Mystery Library™ and my free surprise gift. Then send me 3 mystery books, first time in paperback, every month. Bill me only $4.19 per book plus 25¢ delivery and applicable sales tax, if any*. There is no minimum number of books I must purchase. I can always return a shipment at your expense and cancel my subscription. Even if I never buy another book from the Mystery Library™, the 3 free books and surprise gift are mine to keep forever.      415 BPY A3US

| Name | (PLEASE PRINT) | |
|---|---|---|

| Address | | Apt. No. |
|---|---|---|

| City | State | Zip |
|---|---|---|

\* Terms and prices subject to change without notice. N.Y. residents add
applicable sales tax. This offer is limited to one order per household and not
valid to present subscribers.
© 1990 Worldwide Library.

MYS-796

# MEADOWLARK

*First Time in Paperback*

# SHEILA SIMONSON

## A Lark Dodge Mystery

When ex-California book dealer Lark Dodge is cajoled into running a seminar at a local writers' conference, she couldn't know where it would lead her.

Then Hugo Groth, the tenant renting the apartment above Lark's store, is found dead at the organic farm where the conference is being held. Curiously, he is found packed in ice meant for the broccoli harvest.

But the conference must go on—and with it a hunt for a killer with another murder in mind.

**"There is a light touch of humor combined with taut writing and an enjoyable mystery."** —*Mystery News*

Available in June 1997 at your favorite retail stores.

---

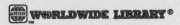 **WORLDWIDE LIBRARY** ®                    WLARK

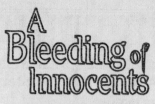

A

# Bleeding of Innocents

First Time in Paperback

## A Castlemere Mystery

## DESPERATE MEASURES...

The Castlemere police force loses one of its own to a hit-and-run. Adding stress to an already understaffed force, a young nurse is brutally murdered in her car with her husband as the only witness. Is there a shotgun killer walking the streets, or is her distraught husband guilty of more than he'll admit?

But after another horrible shooting murder, it's clear there's a serial killer on the loose.

# Jo Bannister

"Bannister keeps the suspense tight as a drum."

*—Publishers Weekly*

**Available in June 1997 at your favorite retail stores.**

NOT FOR SALE IN CANADA.

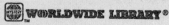

WORLDWIDE LIBRARY®

WBLEED-R

# CYBERKISS

## A Silicon Valley Mystery

*First Time in Paperback*

**MURDER ON-LINE...**

Bernie Kowolsky is scared to death when he arrives at Julie Blake's computer investigations office with a tale of kinky cybersex turned lethal.

When Julie and her partner, Vic Paoli, go undercover as programmers at the high-tech pharmaceutical firm where Bernie works...they arrive just in time to stumble over his body in the parking lot.

Now that their client has become roadkill on the information superhighway, the undercover investigators find themselves in an erotic web of computer treachery, hunting for a devious killer.

## SALLY CHAPMAN

"A well-plotted, riveting must-read." —*Booklist*

Available in July 1997 at your favorite retail outlet.

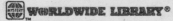